I0532611

Lilah Keeper

and

The Deceiver's Heir

~

Summer V. Schmier

Copyright © 2014 Summer V. Schmier

All rights reserved.

ISBN: 978-0692264713

DEDICATION

For Grandma Tina and Grandpa Alfred. It is of you that I will always dream.

CONTENTS

1 An Unexpected Savior

I guess I could've been born an ordinary person, I thought. *One of those usual people who likes to wake up in the morning, survive the day, and peacefully fall asleep at night. But it isn't really possible with the Gift. And really, what would be the fun in that?*

Dust twirled through golden beams of sunlight above the mossy, thirty-foot high stone walls surrounding the town. The tiny particles shifted playfully through the air, inviting me to chase them. But my mind wandered elsewhere. The smooth gray rocks were packed together so tightly that a breath of wind couldn't have slipped through. Unseen, rows of razor-sharp wire extended ten feet below into the earth. I stared from a distance and couldn't help but imagine each stone as a separate jail bar, wondering *what could possibly* be on the other side, as I did all the time.

There was only one way into the town, and only one way out: through the solid metal gate that stretched just as high as the walls. But nobody was allowed to leave. If any of the townspeople were

1

overly curious and stepped too close to the gate, they were taken away and rarely seen again. Those were the times I hated the most, when innocent people were punished for their natural instincts.

Perching on the white wooden railing on the front porch of my home, I watched the commotion near the gate. An old, clueless man had drifted too near the heavy metal doors and was being beaten and dragged away by two hooded figures, or Deceivers as they were usually called, because they had a skillful way of luring people in and then betraying them.

The man struggled and wailed, explaining he had done it by accident, but he was beaten unconscious and dragged through the town until they disappeared from my view. I wanted to run to him and help; I was sure everybody in town wanted to, but I had learned to restrain myself. One confrontation with the Deceivers was bad enough.

A flashback to two years before wandered across my mind. I was only thirteen, and hadn't yet learned how to control my impulsiveness. Let's just say I never learned to, really. Self-restraint, sadly, wasn't my specialty:

A crowd was gathered near the gate where everyone greeted the leader of the hooded figures, Casimir, as he returned from his visit to the outside world. A silence blanketed the crowd as his clouded white eyes shone madly from out of his scarred, pale face.

"My people," he had said, sitting on an open black carriage pulled with chains by some of the punished townspeople and some of his own Deceivers. He could have easily used horses to pull the carriage, but he enjoyed feeling above everyone else, "I have *returned.*"

The townspeople then pulled their hands together in forced, lifeless clapping. A light fog clung to the air just above the street and floated around Casimir's figure. From out of the crowd, Casimir's wife Lucetta reluctantly stumbled up to meet her husband. She was a sad little thing, and not even a Deceiver.

They were of two different species altogether, it seemed, the Deceivers and the townspeople. Perhaps they were the same on the outside, but on the inside, something caused the Deceivers to become corrupt. They were all blind, but could hear like bats, and all had the same silvery hair.

After the applause had ended, Casimir ordered his carriage-pullers to take him back to his home at the far edge of the town, but one of the punished collapsed to the ground from exhaustion. A nearby Deceiver went to him and drew a metal nightstick, but I couldn't stand to see the man get hurt. I removed myself from among my mother, father, and brother as I stepped between the man and the Deceiver. Although I heard my mother whimper and my father catch his breath with fear, I continued.

"You don't have to do this," I had said, trying to make the collapsed man stand; "give him a chance to breathe." I had said it calmly, but a hint of hesitation escaped on my last word.

The Deceiver sneered, "Move *little girl*, or you'll be punished too."

All was still for a moment until Casimir chuckled, "No, let her

3

stay; this is interesting. What's your name, girl?"

I drew in a breath and glanced around me at the frightened townspeople. "Lilah," I answered.

A cold smile twisted his lips. "Ah yes, Lilah Keeper. Always a *feisty* little thing, weren't you? You remind me of how my daughter Cyra was, before her death..." he trailed off for a second. "However, it's always the feisty that are the most dangerous. You wouldn't want to put your family and friends in danger, am I right? So back down." His words made my sudden rise of courage drop. Although he was blind, I could feel those eyes boring into me, threatening to claw into the depths of my confidence.

"D'you really think that *your* threats scare us? Your *Deceivers* with their *nightsticks* are the only things we're afraid of. That shows cowardice on your part, Casimir," I said, my hands trembling.

The smile on his face then receded and irritation replaced it. A Deceiver approached me but he waved her away. The air was so silent that I wondered if he could hear my heart beating.

"Ha, you're more ignorant than I believed. Haven't your parents taught you anything? This is no way to speak to your *leader*," Casimir snapped. The unconscious man was replaced by a Deceiver and they were ordered to begin pulling the carriage again. "And because of this your family's food supply will no longer exist for the next three years. Good luck surviving."

A strange, fearful glance flickered momentarily across his face, but then he flashed a smirk. This odd jumble of emotion was common with Casimir, but I felt as if nobody else noticed.

He was taken through the streets until I could barely see him, when a strange sight caught my eye. On the back of the carriage was Casimir's son, Revelin as I'd heard he was called, and he was arguing with his father. Just as the carriage turned the corner and disappeared, Revelin glanced in my direction and a look of wonder appeared on his face.

I shook my head to clear the flashback, returning to reality. As the final rays of the sun sank behind the wall, I took one last glance at the uniform suburban houses in the small town and hopped off the railing to go inside. My mother sat in a rocking chair warming herself by the fire, which many would consider weird in warm weather, but I'd grown used to it because I knew it gave her a sense of lively energy—something that she found difficult to come across. She was a dreamer. She hoped for a life similar to that in the storybooks I always read to my brother, one filled with limitless adventures and surprises.

Living in an enclosed town, however, forced her to scrounge for those dreams.

My father sat on a couch near the fire, still in his work clothes. He looked younger when he reclined there, the years of toil sinking behind the warm glow of the flames. Though he loved his job of healing the emotionally sick, he sometimes had difficulty healing himself. I nodded at him, smiling, and at my mother, but I didn't hug or speak to them.

My younger brother then walked into the room, his messy jet-black hair and brown eyes catching the light of the fire as he went to sit on my mother's lap. His plump cheeks and round face made him appear far younger than six. They looked like a photograph sitting in front of the fire, holding each other's hands securely, and my mother's straight golden hair falling around him like a curtain. Andrew's flower-petal lips curled into an innocent smile.

We knew it was disapproved, to speak just before night when the Deceivers were tired, because they hated it. The sound of happy voices irritated them. We were all itching to talk, but we didn't utter a word until night. Most of the Deceivers—except for the advanced ones that patrolled the walls day and night, able to hear a feather drop—would go home to the palace by then, and we could speak without being overheard or watched.

We all sat in silence, waiting, as light disappeared outside and night cloaked the town, and the quiet sound of the Deceivers' footsteps vanished as they returned to the palace.

I went to my father then, and embraced him, hoping his complex thoughts would subside for a while with the comfort of my arms around him. He was a frequent over-thinker, and if nobody tried to stop him, he would often fall into his own mind…sucked into his own thoughts as if into a black hole.

My mother squeezed her arms around Andrew.

"I wait for this moment every night, you know," my mother began, her green eyes flickering, "a moment when we can be free to do whatever we want. It's almost impossible to do anything during the day without being *watched*." She rocked little Andrew back and forth on her lap; he was just small enough to hold. My mother wasn't so strong.

I turned to my father, admiring how he could pull through a day without cursing, admiring his strength of heart. The thing that bothered him most of all was always being under subtle surveillance. "Privacy is very important," he would say, "and those Deceivers don't seem to understand." His short, brown hair and beard were peppered with gray.

"I like these times too, Jane," he said, beaming at my mother with a wild fire in his dark eyes, "but we shouldn't spend it like this. We'll have a feast tonight. What d'you think, Lilah?"

I agreed because I knew those times were rare, those times when my father had enough determination to have a feast of food. Ever since Casimir revoked our food supply a couple of years ago, we were left to find our own source for it, and we had to ask friends for whatever they could spare in the dark of night when the Deceivers were scarcely on the streets. Most of the time I had to go out alone because I was the quickest, but tonight I would have a companion.

My mother and Andrew wished us luck as we each put on a black jacket and quietly slipped out the door. The town appeared ghostly: The night air was cool and the sky was clear with the exception of the gleaming stars and full, white moon, and a thin fog whispered through the streets.

"Go to Alice's house first and then Nico's. Alice may have

enough food in all to give and we don't want to take from Nico's family if we don't have to. I'll see what our neighbors can spare," my father said, mapping out a plan.

"We don't need a plan; just go with your best instinct, and hide if you hear a sound," I said, observing the area to make sure no Deceivers remained on the street. "And dad, be careful."

My father drew his coat closer around his head and ran off into an alley, his shoes padding against the old, stone street. I gazed up at the night sky one last time as my bare feet silently found the cool line of grass along the edge of the similar houses. The green blades spiked out unevenly beneath my feet.

I slid quietly through the alleys and around houses. Though there was nobody I had to hide from that I could see, I felt an occasional shift of disturbed wind or saw an out-of-place shadow. My stomach fluttered nervously…I glanced behind me a few times, having the feeling of being followed.

I stopped walking altogether and stood, observing, as I hid myself behind a solitary lilac tree that served as a marker between the end of the suburbs and the beginning of the way into Casimir's palace, or the Silver Kingdom as it was sometimes called.

The ground beyond where the tree stood turned from old stone into smooth, flat metal that reminded me of the blade of a sword. It spread on for a long way, stretching between the two miles of ground within the walls left and right, and led forward quite a way to the palace doors. The palace was a cruel-looking thing, made of an even shinier silver metal and higher than ten suburban houses stacked upon one another. Two towers with needle tops swayed beside it, and the only light came from a large lamppost that glowed with a blue light just in front of the doors.

There were a few other metal houses spread around it, shaped like triangles, creating the Deceivers' homes. The dark sky above it hung motionless, its spirit imprisoned. It seemed to be calling out, begging to be freed.

A couple of Deceivers sleepily marched around the palace, but they were so far away I didn't fear being caught. A few rays of the blue light faintly shone on the white houses beside me as I turned into one last alley before I reached Ali's house. I liked to think I was good at that, finding my way through the tight passages between houses, because it seemed I could rarely find pride in anything else. I had some difficulty at first, but after nearly three years, I had mastered it.

When I reached Ali's house, she was already waiting for me at the door. Her shoulder-length auburn hair looked darker in the black of night. Though she was fourteen, a year younger than I, her face already appeared as a mother's might: tired, wise, and peaceful from many years of caring for her four younger siblings and parents, who had gone through so much trouble with the Deceivers that they were rarely at home. But they had to be taken care of when they were. Ali's parents were regular patients at my father's hospital.

As I stood for a moment and observed her, I realized she was like one of those metal wind chimes that my mother sometimes set on the porch in the warm weather. Ali's voice always had a soft tingling innocence to it that suggested vulnerability, but if somebody tried to corrupt her, they would realize that she was much stronger than they could have imagined.

"Lilah," she whispered in that light, witty tone, "hurry, come in."

Her home looked almost identical to mine, even on the inside, as they all were. I said hello to all four of her younger siblings who scampered around the kitchen and living-room playing, and gave a hug to Alice Hale, one of my two best friends.

"Are your parents back?" I asked, noticing they weren't in the room. I knew the answer anyway, but at least she would know I cared.

"No," she replied, somewhat sadly, but then looked to her wild sisters and brother, "but I can see why they'd rather be at the mental hospital."

I laughed softly, careful not to sound insulting, as she tried to calm down her yelling brother, but then gave up and laughed too. She then went to the kitchen and returned to me with a small sack containing half a chicken and some fruit. Even though her parents were gone, Casimir still allowed Ali's family to receive their food ration. I could see that look in her almond-shaped, blue eyes, that look that told me she wished she could have gotten more.

"Thanks, Ali. Really, it's perfect. I don't think I'll need to ask Nico for anything now," I told her, thinking of Nico and how his family always had trouble getting enough food for themselves.

Still, I lingered there for a moment, knowing what she was going to say next.

"Visit him though. Will you? You know, make sure he's alright after that problem with the Deceivers," she said, concern flashing across her face and pressing her thin lips into an even thinner line. I was always prepared for that question, though surprised at what she said after it.

"What happened with the Deceivers? Did he tell a joke again?" I asked, though it was probably just the usual incident where Nico laughed loudly or said something funny in their presence. That's what the Deceivers hated the most, humor; or at least it seemed that way.

Ali paced nervously in front of me, occasionally flicking her eyes towards her younger siblings who attempted catching lightning-bugs that ventured near the single open window.

"He didn't tell you? He was caught trying to sneak into the Silver Kingdom on the back of one of Casimir's carriages," she paused for a minute and sighed. "You know how my parents haven't been home for about half a year now? Nico was so angry that Casimir would keep them there for so long, he wanted to try to find them. I know he was trying to help, but I wish he hadn't."

I sighed, though I wasn't surprised, because Nico was often trying to do things that he was too clumsy to accomplish, or that were simply too big a task for him to handle alone. "It's all going to work out, I promise. He really cares about you," I reassured her, opening the door to leave.

"I know, and I care about him too. And Lilah, you will go to him, won't you?" She said just as I was about to disappear.

I smiled and laughed quietly, "Don't I always?" It was true; Ali asked me every time to go to him, and I always did. I admired that about her, the ceaseless caring for people, and how she could hardly find a flaw in anyone except for the Deceivers. It was amazing how someone could be so humble.

The wooden door to her house creaked behind me as I closed it and prepared myself to go to Nico's house, as the quietest sound caused me to hold my breath and glide behind the railing on Ali's small front porch.

There was a distant sound of feet clumsily stumbling on the stone street and I waited silently as a silhouette passed. It was a Deceiver, probably drunk as I could tell by the way she walked, and her blind eyes rolled crazily within her skull. I dared not breathe until she was gone, but she stopped for a moment and listened, her head tilted toward me. I felt my heartbeat quicken, and I tried to calm myself the best that I could, but when I took a breath, I knew it was too late.

The Deceiver's lifeless eyes shot in my direction and a smile revealing jagged yellow teeth crawled upon her face. I ducked down and dove between two of the white railing bars, sprinting towards a dark alley. I could hear the Deceiver behind me, her heavy footsteps easily distinguishable.

"Come here, cutie, I won't hurt you," she hissed, her voice sounding eerily similar to Andrew's. That was how they deceived people: by mocking the voice of someone they loved. It was rather cruel, really.

Her voice was flowing, sweet, and thick like honey as all of the Deceivers' voices were, trying to draw me in, but I denied it. Normally she would have caught me in a matter of seconds, because that's what they trained for, but she was greatly intoxicated and tripped on every stone that jutted out unevenly.

I could feel her just on my heels, her icy breath prickled the back of my neck, and I could see her pale face glowing in the moonlight from the corner of my eye. I tried to swallow but choked on the dryness of my throat…she was right behind me…faster, I had to run faster. She lunged her arms forward, attempting to grab me, but I ducked and she toppled onto the ground as I continued tearing through the alleys.

I was near Nico's house then, but I slowed to a stop in the shadow of a house to catch my breath and made sure the Deceiver was no longer on my trail. My muscles relaxed as I heard nothing but the wind, and turned to go the rest of the way. For not even a minute, I was alone. I heard it first, and then felt it: the Deceiver's laugh and her arms squeezing around me, threatening to break my back.

Releasing a quick scream, I struggled against her grip. How had she gotten to me so quickly? I resented her, I resented them all, from Casimir to every last Deceiver.

A forceful yell then suddenly sounded from behind us, and a long, metal object collided with the Deceiver's shoulder and side of her head. Immediately she released the grip on me and fell to the ground unconscious. I gasped and choked on my breath, watching as a bruise quickly formed on her neck, her mouth hanging open and her eyes motionless.

My eyes shot toward the direction of the person who hit the Deceiver, but there was nothing to be seen. Confused and curious, I ran to the side of the house, searching for the rescuer.

Without noticing me, a boy was sauntering away through the alley, a metal nightstick in his hand. Immediately I recognized him as one of those people who *saunter* instead of walk. *Walking* wasn't good enough for him.

"Who are you?" I asked as he turned to face me.

He sighed as he walked nearer, acting as if he had better things to do than talk to me. I picked at my memory—I had seen him before, I was sure of it; something in his blue eyes seemed familiar. He couldn't have been much older than I, seventeen maybe, and he had a cocky air about him.

He was silent for a moment, taking in the sight of me with a mischievous smile on his lips. "I think a 'thanks' wouldn't hurt. I'm used to more praise, you know," he said, and I was suddenly annoyed.

"I could have gotten rid of her myself. It's not like I *asked* you for help," I replied, turning to go, "but thanks, I guess."

Before I could leave, he blocked my way. "Is that it? Usually those I help bow at my feet or something, to show they're thankful. I'm Revelin Ridger, Casimir Ridger's son." He beamed stupidly as

I processed what he said.

So he was Casimir's son, the boy I had seen nearly three years ago on the back of the carriage.

I shook my head because he was still standing there, expecting me to bow down to show my gratitude. I brushed past him, and as I made my way to Nico's house, he followed behind me without stopping. Finally, just as I was on Nico's steps, I turned to face him.

He stood there at the foot of the stairs, with his hands in his dark short's pockets and the same smile on his lips: one corner of his mouth was raised boldly and his eyes were lazily droopy. His shoulders were set back and his chin was elevated, and I found it incredible how one person could be so egotistical. I had heard many bad things about him from other kids, but I never really believed them because I knew that Nico had been friends with him at some time.

"Is there some reason why you're following me? I already said thanks, but I'm not going to kiss your feet or anything," I said, wondering if he would ever leave.

He laughed then; actually, truly, genuinely laughed. It was a bit higher-pitched and freer than his usual deep voice. "You're weird, you know that? And I just wanted to tell you…" His voice dropped off for a moment and he seemed to be gazing into his memory. "I liked what you did back then, two years ago. The way you stood up to my father. I could never do it, but after I saw you do it, I knew I could. So I just wanted to say, 'thanks.' I was out walking and I saw her chasing you, so I decided to help."

Looking at him, I wondered how he could have been Casimir's son. He wasn't blind, he wasn't cruel, and his skin wasn't even that pale. Unlike the Deceivers' silvery hair, he had wavy, dark, chocolate-colored hair that fell thickly around his head. But then I remembered his mother, and how he looked a lot like her, and how I would never understand why she would have married Casimir out of all people.

I wanted to say a thousand things, but all that came out was, "You're welcome. And I'm glad you're not what I thought you were." I said, confusing him.

We turned simultaneously and just as my hand clenched the doorknob, I heard his voice again, from farther away, "And Lilah, wipe that scowl off your face. You're not going to make any friends with it." His laugh bounced through the street as he disappeared into the darkness. I guess I had been scowling, but that was because I was worried about Nico and his Deceiver problem.

I murmured insults back, but I knew he was too far away to hear me. Maybe Revelin wasn't so bad after all; definitely annoying…but there was something within him that made him seem so different from his father.

2 The Dreamer

My thoughts immediately jumped back to Nico as I opened the door to his house and went in. I dropped the sack of food Ali had given me by the door so he didn't think I came for extras.

The living-room was dark except for one candle, and the hallway that led back to the bedrooms seemed to be the most lighted area in the house, so I went back to his room. I noticed his parents fast asleep in their bed before I quietly sneaked past and went to see Nico.

I carefully closed the door behind me as I went to sit beside him on the bed. He was deeply asleep, I could barely see his chest rise and fall with his steady breaths. A short, melted candle flickered on his night table and I suddenly thought of Casimir and how he didn't allow electric lights in the town because he liked the darkness.

I watched as each ray of candlelight glinted off Nico's messy straw-colored hair and illuminated his strong but sweet facial features. I placed my hand on his and smiled, happy to have him as a friend.

Deciding not to wake him because he looked so peaceful, I planted a soft kiss on his forehead, my lips brushing his rough skin, and stood to leave. My hand turned the doorknob but I stopped when I heard him moan and sit up.

"Whoa, come back," he said, grinning at me, "can I have another one of those?" He closed his eyes and puckered his lips, and I laughed and collapsed onto the bed beside him. Though we were the same age, something about the innocence of his face in that moment made him seem younger.

"In your dreams," I replied, looking into his brown eyes and laughing again. I sat dazed for a second, my words reminding me of the Gift my father passed down to me…*in my dreams*…but I told myself now was not the time to think of it. We were silent for a minute, embracing the peace. I couldn't help but sneak a few glances at him; for some reason I wanted to move closer.

"Ali told me about how you tried to find her parents. That was stupid and dangerous, Nico, but brave. I wouldn't have expected you to do that," I said as I watched his family's pet black cat leap onto the bed and settle between us. Its piercing silver eyes flashed about the room as if watching an invisible bird fly above our heads.

"It's the best I could do; you know how much she misses them. Even if they would just be more of a burden for her, I had to see her really, truly happy for once. It's rare these days, to see her smile," he said, his expression distant while, I guessed, he thought of Ali.

"She's doing fine; I went to see her before I came here," I said.

He nodded, and then looked confused. "If you were just at her house, why did it take you so long to get here?"

I thought for a moment, imagining what time it could be and how my father was probably worried because I'd been gone for a long time, and then Nico's stare caused me to surface back to reality.

"I was chased, by a drunken Deceiver. But she didn't catch me because *Revelin*, of *all* people, knocked her unconscious. It was strange that he was following me, but he said it was because he wanted to thank me for giving him the courage to face Casimir. Why are you friends with him?"

Nico grinned, with a look in his eyes that told me he knew something I didn't. But then his face returned to its usual expression as he explained, "Oh, well, because he really isn't that bad. People say he is, but he's actually not. I think everyone is just afraid of him."

I nodded, agreeing, but then told him I had to leave because my father was waiting. We stood up from the bed and I stared at him for a moment, watching his eyes reflect the candlelight, before he swiftly, smoothly drew me into a hug, his arms wrapping around my shoulders. We stood there for quite a long while, neither of us speaking, listening to each other's heartbeats, savoring a moment that rarely could happen. A strange tingle of excitement prickled my skin as he squeezed me tighter, but the peace was broken by a sound of feet shuffling outside of his room.

We broke away from the embrace just as a knock sounded on his closed door. "Nicodemus Bertha Aljoy, who are you talking to in there?" his overly-protective mother demanded from behind the door.

Nico's cheeks flushed a bright pink as I suppressed a laugh. "You see…Mum wanted a daughter named Bertha, but she got a son instead, so she had to put that name somewhere…" he mumbled.

"WHO'S IN THERE?" she squealed, trying to twist the locked doorknob.

"Quickly, go out the window," he whispered as I sprang to it, opened it, and began climbing out. "Uh," he said nervously back to his mother, "Just the cat, mom."

As I landed on the ground outside his window, I quieted myself and began my way back to my house. Bertha…all these years and I never knew his middle name.

The air was cooler then, and the moon lit up the sky. A few strips of clouds were scattered across the night sky like seaweed in an ocean. At least, what I thought seaweed might look like. I had only seen a picture of an ocean that a friend had given me, but never a real one.

How long had I been gone? Then I remembered: I left the sack of food from Ali at Nico's house, but I was not going back; it was too late. Infuriated, I slid stealthily through the alleys. My footfalls were louder because I felt careless, too absorbed in thought. When I reached home I saw my father still sitting on the front porch, his face cupped in his hands.

I tapped him on the shoulder. He looked up and broke into a smile. "Oh, Lilah!" He said, standing and leading me inside, "Thankfully you're alright. I thought you might have been caught." He, at least, had not returned empty-handed. The neighbors must have been generous for one night. Proudly, he dumped the contents of his bag onto the kitchen table as my mother and Andrew welcomed us back, happy nothing bad had happened.

We ate a full meal of roasted ham, rice, and fresh blueberries. I put Andrew to bed telling him his favorite bed time story for the hundredth time. I got up and started for the door.

"Lilah, wait," Andrew called eagerly, sitting up in bed.

I turned around questioningly.

He tugged at his shirt collar nervously. "The stories you tell me are *real*…right?"

I felt a lump in my throat…I knew that he was going to ask that question eventually, but I hoped it wouldn't be soon. The plain wooden frame of the bed creaked as I sat back down beside him.

"Do you want them to be real?" I asked, smiling.

He nodded crazily.

"Then, you don't need to ask me if they are or not. The most exciting things are those that are unknown," I said.

Andrew's mouth hung open as if he wanted to speak, but he was too lost in thought and confusion. Without another word, he settled back into the bed, and I left before he could ask another question. I returned to my room, preparing myself to go through my nightly routine.

For regular people, the most difficult challenges are not lying, not cheating, and not giving in to temptation. For me, the most difficult thing to do is sleep. Because of my father's Gift that was passed down to me, I have to wake up every hour during the night, so that if I dream, nothing bad happens. I despise doing it, but it's a sacrifice I have to make…a responsibility I have to own.

I've trained myself to wake for a few seconds every hour, and I fell into my first hour of sleep, thankful but also disappointed that it was dreamless. I love having dreams, but they are too dangerous. It was like drifting into a world of fantasy and the impossible. It was my escape, but what is an escape when I'm not allowed to run?

Each hour I awoke and successfully kept the dreams at bay, until the hour before dawn when one slipped into my consciousness.

I dreamed about receiving my Gift from my father. I remembered how, when I was ten years old, he told me it was time and a strange sensation came over me. An endless field stretched around us, except for the single lilac tree under which we were standing. One half of the field contained shadowy, wilted grass, while the other radiated with fresh grass. My father explained to me what the Gift was, staring up into the purple-blossomed lilac tree.

"Lilah, there are many people in this world," he said in my dream, his voice soft and hazy, "but there's only one that can have the Gift. It was first given long ago, during a time that no one seems to remember, to help the recipient during a great war.

"The man was struggling, and given a Gift stronger than any army. He could turn his nightly dreams into reality if he chose, and even bring the dead back to life, if he dreamt it. At first, it was difficult, and he accidentally dreamt up volcanoes that destroyed innocent villages because he didn't know how to control it. It's dangerous, Lilah. You have to be wise and avoid dreams at all costs, even if they seem tempting. People say that most things are impossible, but not for you. For you, the word *impossible* does not exist."

His explanation was difficult to believe, though. It wasn't complex enough. Where did the Gift come from? Who gave it to the man?

"The Gift was then passed onto his child, and his child's child, and so on for many generations until it came to me, then you." In my dream, he then turned to face me.

"It might be difficult at first, but you'll get the hang of it soon enough. First, just make it simple. Dream of a sunny day," he said, and I obeyed. The clouds vanished and a warm sun gleamed in their place. But it all seemed too simple, I couldn't really believe him.

"If you had this ability before me, why didn't you use it to try to escape from the town?" I asked, the dreamland around me fading.

"I…I couldn't Lilah. I was too…afraid. I never quite grasped the power of the Gift, and I feared I would destroy more than I wished to. And many hundreds of years ago, my great- grandfather knew Casimir's great-grandfather. They were best friends, in fact. But soon Casimir's great-grandfather found out about the Gift and grew jealous. He wanted it for himself, but as you know, that's not possible. So he and many of his friends and family tried to capture my great grandfather. Having the same fear that I do, he didn't want to use the Gift in any way. Out of hatred, however, he accidentally dreamed one night that all the people trying to capture him went blind and turned into the ghastly Deceivers.

"Unable to see, Casimir's great-grandfather and his people had a wall built around this town so that my great-grandfather couldn't escape. Since none of them could see, they could never find the one with the Gift out of all of the townspeople. The blind, cruel Deceivers, are still, to this day, searching for the Gift. That is why no one ever tried to escape, because we feared we would be captured or killed. You have the Gift now, Lilah, be careful and use it wisely. And, whatever you do, avoid dreams."

I watched as he wandered away into the half of the field with fresh grass and the dream became fainter and fainter until it turned to something I couldn't quite understand. The scene changed and I could slightly see blazing flames licking and melting something metal.

I woke with a start the next morning, the golden sun peering through my window and glinting off particles of dust that danced through the air like minute ballerinas. I took a deep breath and felt angry at myself for dreaming. I prayed that nothing bad had become reality. The fact that the dream was innocent, though, reassured me. I didn't dream about death or destruction, so nothing bad could have happened. But what were those flames burning, at the end of the dream?

I sat up in my bed and gazed into the mirror on the wall across from me. My pale green eyes stared back. A defined face and full lips caught the sunlight, but the dark shadows always beneath my deep-set eyes clearly indicated my lack of sleep. Not to mention I looked like a manic murderer half the time because of how dark they were.

The small strand of braided hair that I always wrapped around my hairline and the top of my head like a crown was loose and messy. As I redid it, I stared at the strange, circular scar on my right collarbone…remembering how I had gotten it long ago from falling onto a stray piece of metal that jutted out from the ground near the boundary. My turned-in knees and long, slightly bowed legs stretched beneath me as I stood, listening for a while, noticing how unnaturally quiet it was, how silently the air drifted through my room.

Confused, I dragged open the door and went out into the hallway, expecting to hear Andrew's or my mother's voice, but none came. I checked their rooms. They were empty. So, I went to look.

As I went through the front door, I saw my family speaking with a group of Deceivers including Casimir himself. My stomach dropped as if filled with lead. I recognized one Deceiver as the woman who had chased me the previous night, and her blind eyes flickered in my direction as I neared them.

My mother looked terrified. She protectively held onto Andrew's hand so tightly he eventually whimpered with pain. Casimir glared ahead and I realized it was the first time I had seen him off his wretched black carriage.

Why were they here? Did the Deceiver know who I was? I had heard rumors from townspeople about how they could identify a person from something as small as a vocal sound. She seemed to be glaring into me, and her head cocked to the side as she listened to each step I took.

Casimir smiled so sweetly at me that my skin crawled. The morning light shone feebly over the neat rows of houses and then seemed to die altogether when it reached his face. He had deep creases and wrinkles lining his shallow eyes, and shadows seemed to have taken permanent residence in the hollows of his cheeks. His silvery hair, smoothed down on top, just reached his shoulders. He had an odd look of endless fatigue, as if he had lived hundreds of years without sleep, but that look was quickly overcome by a look so harsh that Andrew began whimpering again.

"Hello Lilah, what a pleasure it is to meet you again," he laughed so shrilly, trying and failing to sound cheerful, that I jumped with surprise.

Before I replied, I made my voice low and raspy, so the female Deceiver wouldn't recognize me from my scream the previous night.

"I can't say the same," I replied. The other Deceiver strained her ears on my every word. She looked like a ghost standing there, her skin so pale with the gray hood draped around her face to shield it from the sunlight.

Casimir's cruel grin broadened as he heard my reply. "You still have that defiant streak in you, I see. It's a shame, because I've heard you're such a pretty thing. I wish I could see you to confirm it." He stepped closer to me and stroked my cheek with his bony hand. Immediately, I smacked his hand away and stepped back.

I wondered who had told him that, Lucetta maybe, or Revelin. Maybe one of those mixed-race Deceivers, the ones that weren't blind because they were half townsperson. Surprisingly, his remark angered me, which was hard to do.

"Why are you here?" I demanded, desperately wishing he would leave, "What do you want?" Though I had been keeping my voice deep, it rose to its regular pitch on my last word, and I glanced wide-eyed at the Deceiver, but she hadn't noticed.

"Well, Timoria," he answered, addressing the woman Deceiver who had chased me, "tell them what happened last night."

Coughing to clear her throat, Timoria pulled back her hood to reveal a bush of curly silver hair and I realized she was actually quite young. She flinched from the heat of the sunlight on her face…Deceivers wore hoods to avoid sunlight.

"There was a curfew breaker last night," she began, her voice sugary and quiet. "I almost caught her. And I would have, if only I hadn't become unconscious." She stumbled nearer to me, clearly still recovering from a hangover. After patting the top of my head, she nodded, as if she had just confirmed something.

"Yes, she was your height, but certainly not as deep-voiced. Yours sounds strained, though. Is that natural?" Timoria, obviously meaning it as an insult, grinned, revealing her yellow teeth, and her liquor-scented breath drifted to my nose. A look came over her that made it obvious she knew I was the girl she had almost caught.

"Yes, it's natural, just like that bump on your head must be."

She scowled and turned on her heel to face Casimir.

"This isn't the girl," she hissed to him, and he looked displeased. My eyebrows rose, surprised she hadn't told him the truth, because hiding things from Casimir was worse than killing him, and someone like Timoria should clearly have known that.

They turned and began to walk away. Once Casimir and the other Deceivers were out of earshot, Timoria spun around and dashed back toward me. "Lucetta asked me to protect you," she said. Then, she returned diligently to Casimir's side. My family, muttering about the audacity of the Deceivers, went back into the house. My father patted my shoulder as he passed and my mother squeezed my hand, thankful that we weren't caught. I stood there for a moment as I thought about Timoria's words.

Lucetta. I had to search my memory for a while until I could remember Lucetta's face. She was Casimir's wife, and perhaps she was kinder than her reserved, fearful manner suggested. She had never done anything bad to the townspeople or anything stupid—except to marry Casimir—but I even heard she did that because her father forced her to so he could get a larger supply of food.

I still didn't understand, however, why she had asked Timoria to keep me safe by lying to Casimir. I hardly knew Lucetta, but as I pictured her face, my thoughts went to Revelin, and how they had the same dark hair, and then I guessed why. Revelin had thanked me for showing him that his father could be challenged, and probably had asked Lucetta to spare me. But why, then, would Timoria ever obey fragile Lucetta?

3 Delvadar Alley

As morning crept into midday, I wandered toward Delvadar Alley, which in addition to a few shops, contained the town's only school. There was never an official name given to the town. Some called it Delvadar after the street, while some simply called it The Town. Only about seven hundred people lived here, and it bloomed in warm weather; the kids ran through the streets, their fingers sticky with sugary candy, and the warm air breathed through the alleys as if chasing away the cold. The situation with Timoria and Casimir still clouded my mind

I turned the corner onto Delvadar Alley and into the swarm of people weaving around as they hunted for things to buy. The first store to the right, Talia's Tunics and Trinkets, contained hundreds of different colored clothes. Beside it were Lellagon's Hospital, where my father worked; Outside World Oddities, which had a few things supposedly from the World Beyond the Walls; and the Bank of Seil, which was the only store owned by the Deceivers.

The Bank of Seil dominated every other store in the town.

There was always a line of people standing outside the door waiting to receive their share of Verras, the currency of the town. A Verra was a flat, shiny, triangular sheet of silver metal…about the size of an egg…with Casimir's face imprinted on the front. In order to get food, people had to exchange their Verras at the bank, which also served as the food market.

My eyes lingered on Delvadar's Delights candy shop, the first store along the left side of the street, which was overflowing with townspeople of every age. I neared the colorful front doors and caught sight of the owner, Louis Collioure, as he handed a lollipop to a smiling customer. Louis was unlike any of the townspeople: He was captured by Casimir from a distant place in the World Beyond the Walls when he was just eight years old.

Twenty years ago, Casimir was abroad searching for a source of entertainment for the children in the town, and found Louis and his parents who owned a candy store. Without hesitation, he secretively kidnapped the young Louis and brought him to Delvadar where he was forced to open the shop with the help of a few townspeople. Though he was forbidden to speak to anyone about the World Beyond the Walls, Louis gave subtle hints to those who were curious.

I was five when I first met Louis, and he instantly recognized me as what he liked to call the curious, trouble-making type. Or, as he would say, "zee curious, trooble-making type." The picture of an ocean which I hid in my room and so often stared at was a gift from him, which he discreetly taped to a box of candy that I bought, with the word "ocean" written above it. Throughout the years, he had also given me pictures of forests, deserts, and animals, all of which he sketched from memory.

The now twenty-eight-year-old Louis was one of my good friends. I couldn't resist the grin spreading from ear to ear as I crossed the cobble-stone street to Delvadar's Delights. All of the shops along the street were made of mossy wood on the outside, because Casimir didn't feel like wasting any of the precious metal out of which all his palace was crafted.

A cheerful tinkling of bells echoed through the small shop as I pushed open the orange and gold stained-glass front door. Everywhere children and adolescents faced the many shelves as they filled their hands with fistfuls of assorted candies. One of Ali's brothers, chubby, red-haired, six-year-old Henry, almost rammed into me as he dove for a quickly-emptying barrel of apple-sized lemon drops. Ali spotted me from behind Henry and gave me a hug.

I was about to tell her about the situation with Timoria and Casimir, but before I could speak Louis spotted us. He swerved quickly and made his way through the crowd, his golden-brown hair flying back and his tall body easily distinguishable. Louis was always so happy, even though I couldn't imagine how much he missed his family.

"Ali and Leelah, 'ow great it eez to see you again! Come to zee back room so we can get away from zis noise," said Louis, grabbing one of Ali's hands and one of mine, and leading us through the crowd.

The din of the shop diminished as Louis pulled us into the small room at the back of the shop, and closed the door behind us. I knew the room well, this probably being my hundredth time standing in it, and I instinctively closed the red velvet curtains over the single window. Being watched by Deceivers was what I needed to avoid if I was going to tell them about Timoria and Casimir.

Four old, squashy red armchairs faced each other in the center of the room and dozens of candy- filled barrels lined the walls. To one side stood the cooking area where Louis made the candy. Ali and I collapsed into the armchairs beside each other and she freely ate the chocolates that were in a wooden bowl on a table, but I didn't feel like eating after seeing Casimir up close. That wrinkly face was enough to crack a mirror.

Though it was daytime, the curtains blocked the light so Louis lit a candle and placed it on the table beside the chocolates. He sighed with relaxation as he fell into an armchair across from us, his tawny eyes sparkling in the yellow candlelight.

Louis was rather handsome, but he never seemed to pay any attention to nor showed any care about his appearance. A sharp jawline and contagious smile made him come off as powerful but kind. Whenever he spoke to someone, it was always with rapt attention, though he was quite forgetful and oblivious sometimes.

He had a keen interest in things that others would consider odd, such as what day of the week, month, and year it was (which nobody ever knew); when Casimir planned to next visit the World

Beyond the Walls; and which direction was south.

Shadows looped around the walls of the room, hiding the barrels of candy and Louis's bed and belongings, and I almost forgot about the crowd that was just outside the door. During the day, Louis had a few shop assistants, so he didn't need to worry about helping people and selling the candy.

Ali and I glanced at each other, each of us obviously wanting to talk to Louis about something, but not knowing who should start. There were so many questions about the World Beyond the Walls that Ali and I didn't know where to begin. But before we could speak, Louis seemed to have read our minds.

"I know zat you're going to ask about zee World Beyond zee Walls," he said, his smile fading for a minute as he closed his eyes in concentration, "but I fear zat I 'ave alreedy revealed too much. Zee Deceivers are always suspeecious of me; zey enter my store at least feefty times a day."

My hopes would have disappeared if it weren't for the fact that I knew Louis so well. He always started by saying that he revealed too much, but really he was so eager to leap into descriptions that he had to start by denying it, to keep himself calm. Ali and I pretended to look disappointed, and immediately Louis shot into the state where his eyes appeared glazed: his story-telling state. He was determined to make everybody happy, and he knew that what we wanted was something that only he could supply.

"Very well, eef you must force me to tell you, zen zere eez no

avoideeng it," he said, and Ali and I winked at each other and
beamed, "Where to begeen? Zee lions! 'Ave I already told you
about zem? Beauteeful creatures, strong and noble—"

"The lions sound amazing, Louis;" Ali said quickly, trying not
to interrupt, "you've told us about them before. But what I've
really been wondering is…are there a lot of other people out there?
And where do they live? And what—"

"Not so pushy, Ali," Louis said gently, causing Ali to blush.
"So you want to know about zee people? Well…zat eez zee most
deeficult subject to talk about. People are not easy to describe.
Describing a person eez like trying to describe zee taste of water.
But yes, zere are zousands—maybe even millions—of people in
zee World Beyond zee Walls. Most of zem live in 'ouses very
seemilar to zee ones zat you live in. Some are not so fortunate;
some are very rich. I don't know too much about zee continents
and countries, becuss I was taken away at such a young age—"

"What's a continent?" I interrupted, unable to contain myself.

"Leelah and Ali, I always deed admire both of your
unleemited curiosity, but please let me speak.

"A continent eez a great area of land. Reemember I told you
about zee oceans? Zere are quite a few oceans and continents, but I
can't recall how many." Louis lowered his voice to a whisper and
nervously flashed his eyes toward the door, "Zere are so many
zings zat you will never understand, so many zings zat I cannot
describe to you: zings like zee feeling of sand, zee smell of zee
ocean breeze, zee exhilaration of seeing a wild animal in zee

forest, and zee sound of *music*."

"But *why* Louis? *Why* haven't these people found us? Why haven't they tried to *free* us?" Ali asked, hanging onto Louis's every word just as I was.

For a moment the wonderful glaze vanished from Louis's eyes, and they were downcast as he leaned forward in his chair and rested his elbows on his knees as his hands covered his face. A continual distant sound of tinkling came from the shop as the front door opened and closed. The short candle on the table flicked as Louis puffed out a long breath.

"I don't know," he said simply.

I wasn't convinced, though, and one look at Ali told me that she wasn't either. Wouldn't Louis have remembered at least coming into the town? Wouldn't he have remembered where it was?

"Where are we, Louis? D'you know which continent we're on? Which ocean we're closest to? And which continent did *you* come from?" I pressed him. However, I regretted asking as soon as the words left my mouth. When Louis removed his hands from his face, a couple of tears were twinkling under his eyes. Ali was about to stand and comfort him, as she was a natural comforter, but he wiped the tears away immediately and pretended they were never there.

"Never mind, this is too much," I said shamefully. "I'm sorry, I-I shouldn't have pressed so much. Thanks for telling us as much as you did, Louis, really; Ali and I could never comprehend how much you miss your home. C'mon, let's go try to find Nico; I'm sure he has a great story to tell us about how he made fools of the Deceivers—"

"No!" Louis said, urging us to stay seated. "It eez okay; I want to tell you. Well…when I was captured and taken 'ere, zee journey was too jumbled for me to reemember. I honestly 'ave no idea where in zee world we are right now. 'Owever, I *do* reemember zee place where I was born. Eet was on a continent called Europe, in a country called France.

"Sadly I cannot reemember much about eet. My long-term memory eez very bad, as you know. But I do know zat it was very deefferent from where we are now. Zis place 'as strange, constantly changing weather."

Louis stood from his armchair, parted the curtains an inch, and peered out into the town. His hands were folded behind his back and his posture was very rigid, as if he expected to be kidnapped again at any moment. He never showed this side of himself to anyone except Ali, Nico, and me.

"You'll be able to see…'France' again," I said, trying out the new word. "I promise you that. We *will* find a way out, even if I die trying."

Louis turned away from the window and grinned again, his usual happiness easily bubbling over his sorrow. "Your curiosity, Leelah, will get you far. For most people, imagination eez but fantasy and zings zat do not exist. But some imaginations, like yours, are unique. You see, imagination eez zee key to surviving all zat eez real."

At first I thought he was referring to the Gift, and how it can make the products of my dreams become reality, but then I realized Louis was talking about something else entirely. *Imagination is the key to surviving all that is real.*

"Lilah's right, we *will* find a way to get you back to France. But Louis, something that you said about the outside world sounds familiar to me. You said that you'd never be able to describe the *sound of music*. But don't we hear music every day…people singing and the chirping of birds?" Ali asked.

Her small frame was comfortably huddled into a ball against the corner of the armchair, her chin resting on her knees and her thick hair fanned across her shoulders. Each reddish-brown lock reflected the warm candlelight, and her dark blue eyes gazed at Louis with full attention.

"Ah, music. No, it eez not just singing. You 'ave never 'eard a piano…a veeolin…a geetar. Zey are called *instruments*," he said, his deep voice filling the entire room.

I racked my memory for what Louis called "music," or what an "instrument" was. The only thing that came to my mind was my mother's voice, gentle and sweet, as she used to sing lullabies to me. For some reason, I felt that that wasn't what Louis was talking about.

"Can you draw a picture of one of those things?" I asked, wanting to know what an *instrument* was.

Louis sat still for a moment, and then jumped up with a crazed look to rummage through a pile of his belongings beside the bed. "Where eez it? Where did I put it?"

Certainly Ali and I had not expected this. Rarely would he draw us pictures, but that had only happened once or twice because Deceivers had been in the candy shop every other time. And because the shop was vacant of any Deceivers a few minutes before, Ali and I had been hoping he would draw a picture.

As Louis reappeared and sat in his armchair, he held something that I had never seen before. It was a long object, made of what seemed like shiny hollow wood, and six metal strings were pulled tightly from one end and down over a hole in the center.

"*Zis* eez a geetar," Louis whispered, thoughtfully swiping his hand over the strings, "We 'ave zem everywhere in what you call zee World Beyond zee Walls. I almost forgot zat I had zis beauty. Casimir gave eet to me because I wouldn't stop pestering 'im for an object from zee outside world. Zis eez zee only object 'e would give to me."

Ali nearly leaped out of her armchair when the first sound of the guitar resonated through the room. I was filled with wonder, but curious as to why Louis hadn't shown it to us sooner. It was a sort of metallic sound, and elegant and powerful at the same time. The sound of the strings vibrated through the hollow wood and through the room, rattling the velvet curtains.

Louis's gleaming pearly teeth could have competed with the brightness of the candle. It was obvious that his love truly lay in music, not in candy-making. His happiness made Ali smile uncontrollably, and I couldn't help but laugh when he stood up and started dancing a jig as he sang and played on the guitar.

When zee morning light fills zee sky

Leelah and Ali arrive

I may never even know why,

But in zem, my happiness lies.

Zee gloom of Deceivers

Can never dim zee believers

And Leelah and Ali

Are my friends 'til I die.

Louis returned to his armchair, placing the guitar on the floor. Ali and I clapped and praised him…the music stopped as soon as it started and I was left drooling for more. It was such an innocent thing…why didn't Casimir allow instruments in the town?

As silence enveloped the room again, I remembered the reason why I wanted to speak with Ali and Louis in the first place.

"I almost forgot to tell you," I said, leaning back in the chair and sighing, "When I was leaving your house, Ali, last night after getting food, a Deceiver named Timoria spotted me. She chased me, and I was almost caught. This morning…Casimir came to my house. He suspected me…I could hear it in his voice…but Timoria lied to him and said I was innocent."

Ali shook her head, clearly relieved that nothing bad had happened, and confused. "I'm sorry, Lilah. But why would

Timoria lie to Casimir?"

"When she was leaving and out of earshot of Casimir, she whispered to me 'Lucetta asked me to protect you.' I couldn't really understand at first…but later I realized why. Remember two years ago, when I stood up to Casimir, and his son Revelin was watching? Revelin was thankful that I showed him that it *was* possible to rebel against his father. So, I'm guessing that Revelin told Lucetta to spare me. The only thing that I *don't* understand, is why Timoria would obey anything that Lucetta asked."

Ali and Louis shrugged, obviously as clueless as I was about the situation. I expected they wouldn't have much reaction, but for an unknown reason, some part of me hoped they might have some clue as to what happened.

"When Casimir's daughter Cyra was alive, Timoria 'ad a very close relationsheep with zee leetle girl and often took care of 'er…perhaps Timoria pities Lucetta for 'aving lost 'er only daughter," Louis suggested.

I shrugged, halfheartedly agreeing with Louis. After another few minutes, Louis said it was time for Ali and me to leave. He said that Deceivers could be entering the shop at any moment. We exchanged goodbyes, and promised to meet again soon.

The bells on the front door jingled as Ali and I stepped onto the street of Delvadar Alley. Evening was approaching, and the worn-down cobblestones beneath our feet reflected the reddish sunlight like hundreds of mirrors. We passed a few other places, such as Outside World Oddities, Neil's Necessities, and the small school, which was closed for the warm weather. Since we had been inside the stores so many times, none of them interested us anymore except for Louis's shop.

The school was unnecessary and specialized in tricks. All the teachers were townspeople, since they needed to have eye-sight, but Deceivers were in every corner of each room, always observing. Everyone was taught how to read, write, and do simple math...but any mention of past events was avoided. My father called it *history*, and apparently it revealed too much about the Outside World. Whenever a question arose about it, the teachers glanced nervously at the Deceivers and said nothing. School was rare, though; we only had it for two weeks every month, and had four months off for warm weather. Casimir had to accommodate some of the townspeople's needs or else someone might rebel.

"I wonder why Revelin's so different from Casimir," Ali said as we dispersed from the crowd on Delvadar Alley and walked along an empty street. "Maybe he got more of Lucetta's qualities instead. But he definitely isn't fearful as she seems to be." Ali's cheeks flushed a pinkish hue as she talked about Revelin, but I didn't know why.

I discreetly glanced around the street, and sure enough dozens of Deceivers were hidden in the shadows of houses and alleys, waiting. Waiting and watching. I wouldn't have even seen them if I weren't looking for them. And they were *always* there.

"I don't know. But one thing's for sure," I whispered so

quietly that only Ali could hear, "If we're ever going to get out of here, Revelin's our only hope."

"What makes you say that? It isn't as if he could force the Deceivers to free us," Ali said.

"He's Casimir's heir, isn't he?"

4 The Reality

A few weeks after the visit with Louis, I made my way into the part of town that was the most peaceful: The old fountain that sat motionless upon the mossy stone on the ground around it. The fountain was some distance from the suburban houses, and a long line of tall, green cedar bushes hid it from view. There was never a soul there, except for a few children sometimes. The adults seemed to have little pleasure in it, only glancing in the direction of the fountain whenever they passed.

I slid through a small opening in the line of bushes and stepped onto the stone. There was hardly any stone left, actually; the ground was mostly moss and grass and a few small purple flowers. The fountain stood as always, the crumbling green-gray rock glistening wet in the warm sun. A fresh, soft breeze rustled the bushes as I swept the top of the pool of water in the fountain with the back of my hand.

My dream about the sunny day a few weeks before must have become reality, because the sun shone so brightly the water seemed like gold. It glinted off the metal belt that wrapped around my waist and lightened the shadows in the plain, baggy lilac-colored garment that fell around me like a dress. It went down to just above my knees and had a wide neckline that went into loose, droopy elbow-length sleeves.

It was soft and comfortable, but every girl was required to wear it, which gave me more reason to dislike it. We were allowed to wear different colors, but they all appeared the same anyhow.

As for the belts, every person in town was given one when they reached the age of thirteen, and given a specific size. The belts, as we had to wear them all day every day, kept us from getting any larger around the stomach, and if we no longer could fit into them, we were punished for eating more food than necessary and decreasing the general food supply. We were checked every few weeks by the Deceivers to see if we still fit into them.

Curious, I put my fingers in-between my stomach and my golden belt and felt all the same angry when I should have been relieved. I was thin and there were about two inches between, which was fine, but I didn't care. I wanted to cut off the horrid thing and eat whatever I desired, but I wouldn't risk my family's being hurt.

How could they be so cold? What happened to love? As I sat on the rim of the fountain with my fingers stroking the water, I thought of that. What happened to that love that I always told Andrew about in stories, the passionate love? I had that for my family, but that wasn't the kind I was thinking about. Sometimes I saw it between my mother and father, but that was it.

I heard the crack of a twig behind me, but before I could turn, a hand touched my shoulder and I uttered a surprised sound between a scream and a grunt. I stood and spun on my heel to find Nico keeled over in laughter and Ali beside him.

"That was an *attractive* sound you made. Definitely got me swooning, head over heels," he said sarcastically as he tried to suppress his laughter, but snorted instead. Ali couldn't help but giggle again as I smiled and rolled my eyes.

"Try to make a joke that's actually *funny* next time, Nico," I replied as the three of us had to hold our breath so as not to be heard having too much fun by the Deceivers that sometimes wandered around on the outside of the bushes.

We sprawled out on the grass beside each other and let the sun warm our faces. Nico was on the other side of Ali and propped his head up with one elbow to look at us. After smiling down at Ali, he whispered something to her that I couldn't hear, and she giggled brilliantly.

I knew Nico loved to make Ali laugh, not only because she appeared happier, but because her whole being seemed to brighten like the rising sun, her skin glowing and her round cheeks flushing with life. However, right then I had a strange feeling in my gut, like irritation, at Ali. Seeing the two of them so happy was a blessing, but for some reason I was bothered. I shook my head, easily releasing those thoughts.

Once all was quiet again, Nico gazed into the distance. "We need to get out of here." I sighed, "if only we could. I want to see what else is out there, like a forest, or an ocean. I want to go *swimming*. Could you imagine what that would be like?"

"I want to see more people," Nico added. It seemed all he ever thought about was people, which made sense because he was so skilled in that area. "But you'd think that they would've found us by now and freed us."

Ali nodded, agreeing. We wanted to talk about it more, as each of us could tell; but we had spoken of the same thing so many times before, and never got any proof, so we silently decided to stop.

The clouds passed, full and white, and I watched them, making sure to remember each detail. Yes, maybe I would be able to come outside tomorrow and see them again, but no cloud is ever going to be the same. They're always different. And sometimes I'm caught between choosing whether or not to take the time to remember them, but what would be the harm?

"Did you dream last night, Lilah?" Ali asked, shaking me out of a daze.

They looked at me curiously, as I never used the Gift purposely or told them that much about it because my father told me to restrain it as much as possible. I, too, wondered what I could do with it, but I didn't dare use it.

"I dreamed of a sunny day," I said, shrugging, "but you know that I can't use it when I want to. I have to avoid dreams as much as I can." I laced my fingers through the long grass around me and took a deep breath, deciding not to tell them about the burning metal object at the end of my dream.

We stayed there for quite a long time, minutes ticked into hours, and conversation arose continually but it was thoughtless. Feeling languid, we were motionless until we heard a voice some way off.

"Ali! Where are you?" It was her little sister Tara, using Ali's voice to find her way through the bushes, her blonde curls bouncing with each step. She stood before us, tears of joy welling in her black eyes.

"They're back, Ali," she said, grabbing Ali's hand, "mom and daddy are back!"

Ali first looked confused, and then erupted into a fit of tears and hazy laughter. Before they whisked through the bushes, Nico offered for us to come see them as well, but Ali stood there for a moment, still as a rock, before she answered.

"If you don't mind, I want to go alone. I mean, I'm happy they're back… but I feel something else, too. The Deceivers have been so…," she said, unable to finish. Just as she turned to go with Tara clutching her hand, I heard her say one last thing, "I'm angry." She had said it so hushed, Nico didn't even hear, or little Tara, but I had heard. And I thought of peaceful, sweet Ali with her blue eyes wet with tears, and how she had never really been angry before, only sad sometimes.

Ali possessed a special kind of courage. She sacrificed so

much of herself for other people that I considered her as one of the bravest people alive.

Nico and I returned to our spots on the grass, moving closer so as to fill Ali's empty space. We lay on our backs, each facing the sky and feeling strange without Ali's presence. I said nothing, waiting to see if he mentioned anything about the sack of food I had left at his house accidentally, or his mother, but he began a conversation on something else entirely.

"Lilah, have you ever felt it?" he asked, his voice seeming to echo through the place. It was so familiar, his voice, so comforting. At first, I had no idea what he was asking, but then it came to me, clear as glass. So he had the same strange thoughts I did, and wondered the same things that crossed my mind, too.

"Felt love?" I asked, though I knew that was what he was asking anyway.

He nodded in response, and suddenly I became aware of him. His broad shoulder, the way it just touched the tip of mine, his right hand just inches from my left one, and most importantly his irregular breaths, so unlike his usual steady ones, were the things I noticed. They made me nervous.

I turned my head to the left to face him, the cool grass compressing beneath my cheek. I watched him for a moment, wondering what he could possibly be thinking of.

"No," I replied, facing the sky again, "other than my family, and you and Ali." I wanted that to be the end of the conversation, but I knew it wouldn't be, because Nico wouldn't stop until he received a full, satisfying answer. We both knew that I didn't answer the right way; he was talking about a different kind of love. "No, Nico, I haven't felt that kind of love yet. We aren't even allowed to feel that way until we're twenty years old. The Deceivers punish young love because they think it leads to rebellion. But I guess if I did feel that way now, I wouldn't deny it," I finally said, shrugging.

He turned his head to face me, his mouth slightly open as if he were about to say something. Choosing against it, he blushed, his shyness overcoming his voice.

"But Lilah," he said suddenly, "You…you're *different*…I…you understand things that other people can't…you understand feelings and thoughts…sorry, that sounded so stupid, I…."

I rotated my head again so we were looking right into each other's eyes, and there was a sudden warm breeze that tingled my cheeks. Nico must have felt it too, because a look appeared on his face that I had never seen before. It was something between longing and uncertainty. He made me feel uneasy…excited…but I was too stubborn to admit it.

We looked at each other for a long time, trying to solve an emotional puzzle, seeming to gaze into one another's minds. Without warning, his left hand brushed gently from my hand, up my arm, and onto my cheek, but I pushed it away quickly. His breathing was so uneven that it made me nervous. The sounds around me—the buzzing of bees and the songs of birds—sounded muffled.

Before anything further could happen, we heard a loud crash from somewhere outside and immediately we shot away from each other. I felt my bare knee scrape on a stone and I stared at Nico in awe, realizing how close we had been to one another, and hoping the crash wasn't a Deceiver who had found us and was coming to punish us for such emotions. The bushes didn't move even a leaf, though, so we stood up and pushed through them to get to the town. Nico protectively grabbed my hand, but I was too distracted to react, so I allowed him to hold on.

The crash had come from a destroyed cart full of apples in front of a house, its white walls splattered with bits of the fruit. I just saw, out of the corner of my eye, a woman running away and screaming. The town seemed so unnaturally still, and that was when I noticed how smoky it was.

We nearly fell to our knees when the first columns of smoke tumbled through the alleys. The air was so thick and warm; it felt like boiling honey filling my lungs. Everything around me quivered with a reddish tint.

Swiftly, I helped Nico to his feet and we made our way through town, but it was deserted. Only when we almost reached the area near the lilac tree that marked the boundary between the Shadow Kingdom and the town, did we hear the euphoric chants floating through the heavy air. As we neared the tree, the heat became more intense, but it didn't affect me. It affected Nico, though, and as we stepped into the mixed crowd of people and

Deceivers standing just behind the border, I noticed it affected them too. Some were coughing, or gasping for air, while others chanted encouraging words while tripping around like drunkards.

The stone street felt like sticky, hot coals beneath my bare feet. Nico and I finally got to the center of the crowd, but couldn't squeeze past the tightly compacted people to see what was going on in front of them. I attempted to ask people around me, but they were too delirious, all seeming to be slowly roasting. As I turned to face Nico, however I saw that he was staring up, his mouth slightly open and his brown eyes seeming to be on fire.

But as I followed his stare, I saw that his eyes weren't the thing on fire. I could just see the tips of the metal kingdom, and large, sharp flames were eating away at them. Without further thought, I ducked down to the ground and crawled on my hands and knees between the legs of the people, eventually reaching the front of the crowd. I stood and absorbed the scene, a feeling of pure shock settling within me.

I now knew what the burning metal in my dream was.

The noise of the crowd slowly faded around me until all we could hear was the sickening sound of screams coming from the metal sludge in front of us. I watched as the remaining Deceivers in the kingdom sprinted and stumbled out, a few of them carrying Casimir on their shoulders. I could just see Revelin in front of Casimir's carriers, running full force toward the crowd. The wave of flames sank down from the towers to the bottom of the kingdom and rolled onto the metal ground, just on the heels of the Deceivers carrying Casimir.

Revelin and a few dozen Deceivers dove into the crowd some way to my left, and were safe, and the flames caught up to the two rear Deceivers carrying Casimir and they ran off screaming and burning. The remaining ones kept their hold on their king, and leaped into the crowd. The fire slowed at the border, staying just feet in front of me, and the people around me shrank backward in fear. The flames soared upward at the border like hundreds of fingers reaching for the sky, screaming into the atmosphere, not daring to cross over into the town. *What had I done?*

Before I could witness another thing, I whipped my head around because I heard my father yelling my name. I screamed back to him, trying to overcome the roar of the crowd. I flashed my eyes in every direction but couldn't see him. I drifted deeper into the crowd and heard the townspeople go into hysteria as the Deceivers knocked them unconscious, and I cringed as everyone pushed me farther and farther away from the Shadow Kingdom.

Finally, I spotted my father to the side of me, an angry look of determination clouding his face. I went to him, somewhat expecting him to hug me or hurry me home, but as he reached me, he did something entirely different.

His hand, clutching a cloth, skillfully whisked up to my mouth and I inhaled deeply, not having enough time to react otherwise. The cloth had a pungent scent on it and I felt so confused at first but then the people's faces around me began to twist and blur. The last thing I remembered before I became unconscious was my father scooping me into his arms and carrying me into the town.

5 Joined By the Enemy

When I woke, my eyes remained closed, for I didn't want to open them into something I didn't understand. I hated it when I couldn't understand something; it made me feel vulnerable. I slowly recalled the events from before I fainted, starting with Nico and the fountain and ending with my father's strange action. Why had he done that to me? He knew that whenever I sleep it's dangerous, so why would he purposefully put me to sleep? I then realized how I had been sleeping, and puffed a sigh of relief because it had been dreamless. I felt so curious that I gave in and deliberately opened my eyes.

The first thing I saw was a faintly glowing candle on the floor. I was lying on my side in a thick bed of moss, and the air smelled earthy and dank. I didn't move, but I glanced around the room, which had rock walls and a ceiling that dripped constantly with water.

I was alone, so I sat up in the moss bed and noticed there was nothing else in the room except for a set of stairs that spiraled upward into the ceiling. Carved neatly out of rock and covered in droopy moss, they represented long hours of toil, and the opening at the top was sealed with what appeared to be a slab of stone. I couldn't help but think something looked familiar about the place, but suddenly I felt trapped. My feet, still bare, lowered onto the wet, cold floor and I nearly slipped as I made my way to the staircase. The dark room, I realized, was lit only by the candle, and I hoped it wouldn't burn out.

Ascending the slick mossy steps, I gradually made it to the top, my loose sleeves soaked and my hair plastered down. I noticed the water drops were more frequent, but I didn't care; I wanted to get out. My fingers scraped along the surface of the stone slab, trying to move it, but I was unsuccessful. Then I recognized the stone, the way it felt on my skin, and the color of it. I was beneath the fountain in that garden-like place that was surrounded by bushes.

A sigh of relief consumed me as I knew where I was. I had never known this place existed, and wonder filled me as I realized it did. The room was beautiful, really. It was peaceful, and patches of ivy and moss grew on the floor and walls, but I still wanted to get out.

I saw a crack at the edge of the stone slab and dug my hands into it. With much time and effort, I eventually slid it over, revealing an opening above. I gazed up and saw that it was night, for the sky was dark and a few stars twinkled weakly. Before surfacing, I took a breath and thought of what could await me.

Deceivers, maybe? A deranged father? But why would I be down here; what could have happened?

Expecting to see somebody waiting for me, I climbed out onto the long grass. The bushes cast eerie, scraggly shadows onto the ground and each leaf seemed to whisper to me in the slight breeze. Rays of moonlight created a brightness that could have competed with daytime, and reflected off the pool in the fountain as I dragged the stone slab back over the hole in the ground.

Though my skin was pinkish from the spring sun, it appeared almost gray as I ducked into the shadows of the bushes. The quietest sound of light footsteps was nearing me, and I wasn't going to be seen again by a Deceiver.

The bushes some way in front of me parted and my father stepped through. I stayed hidden for a moment, wondering if he would try to make me faint again, but the crazed look was gone from his eyes. I sprang up to meet him and he jumped with surprise.

"Oh, Lilah, please don't startle me like that," he said as relief flushed his face.

"Why did you do that to me earlier? Why would you make me faint? You know very well that when I sleep without waking every hour it can be destructive," I said, immediately wanting to know the answer.

The moonlight gleamed off the gray hairs on his head and settled in his hollow cheeks. He had gotten thinner. I could especially tell by the way his belt drooped loosely around his waist, and I knew he was really worried; he always lost weight when he was worried.

"I had to. That fire, it was all caused by you. Do you really think a regular fire could melt metal, Lilah? That fire was especially powerful, and I knew it was from your dream. The reason I made you faint was that whenever the person with the Gift is unconscious, their dream is unable to continue its current action. I used some chloroform from my hospital to put you into a dreamless sleep. Right after you fainted, the fire went away and the palace stopped melting," he explained.

Shocked, I allowed the realization of my actions to flood my mind. A sick feeling settled in my stomach…it was my fault those Deceivers died.

He clenched his hands into fists and pressed them into his thighs as he always did when he was angry. I guess that was where I had gotten the habit from, seeing him do it so often. "You have to learn to control it, keep it steady. Avoid dreams."

I paced around the fountain a few times, running my hand along the smooth edge. "I will, but it takes time! It takes practice, Dad. You of all people should know that. Why did you bring me under there after the fire? You could have just brought me home."

He glanced at the fountain, then nervously at the bushes. "I would have," he began, "but one of the non-blind Deceivers saw me making you faint and they're probably suspicious."

I wanted to tell him that was absurd, but I knew he was trying to help. I found that the pacing only made me dizzy, so I stood in front of him again.

I nodded in reply, and then another thought occurred to me, "This is it, Dad. Really, it could be so simple. I could just try to dream of all the townspeople escaping, or the wall around the town breaking down…it would be so easy…we could be free."

Momentarily closing his eyes, he sighed. "No, Lilah. I forbid you to dream anything." He smoothed his hand over his face in frustration, "I'll tell you a story, alright? When I was about your age, I thought that I owned the world. The Gift made me egotistical, and I didn't obey my father's commands to avoid dreams. I wanted anything and everything I set my eyes on, especially a beautiful woman. Her name was…well that isn't important.

"She had long, dark hair and beautiful black eyes, and such an alluring aura that every boy wanted her. So one night before I went to sleep, I focused on a particular scene of the two of us sitting on the porch outside my house, holding hands. I focused on our feelings—I tried to make her love me. As I fell asleep, my dream happened just as I planned, but then it turned into the opposite of what I hoped: she didn't love me; she despised me. The dream fed on my fear instead of my desire, because my fear was stronger.

"So after I woke, she deeply loved me for a few weeks and we told each other everything. But soon, like in my dream, her feelings changed. Every day since then, whenever I see that woman, she scowls at me with such hatred that even Casimir himself couldn't conjure. Believe me, Lilah, no dream is worth the danger, just as you saw with the fire burning the kingdom."

"But Dad, the woman's name, was it…" I began.

He drew the coat off himself and wrapped it around me, covering my head with the hood, "Enough questions. Casimir's having a gathering tomorrow at the gate; I want you to come, but you are not to be anywhere near us. Stand with people you don't know, but don't talk to anyone. If you don't come, Casimir will notice your absence and that'll prove that you have the Gift. You'll have to sleep here tonight. Please, be careful."

"I'm not afraid, Dad," I said reassuringly, seeing the worry cloud his face. I actually was a bit scared, but I figured one troubled person was better than two. "It'll be fine; they won't even notice me."

He smiled a little as he took something out of his pocket, "Also…I wanted to give this to you. I—I should have given it to you sooner. I'm a fool, a selfish fool… I've had it with me for so long now that it's difficult to part with. But you need it far more than I do."

His fingers slowly fumbled in his pocket until he drew out something that looked like a necklace. Gently placing it in my palm, he closed my fingers around it. As the object left his touch, a look of guilt and longing seemed to have passed over him that I couldn't understand.

"My father gave this to me before he died, and I carried it around with me wherever I went. It's *very* important that you keep this with you at all times, and that Casimir *never* touches it. It's intended to be good, but it's also tempting, and I let it overcome me…I used it to hide my feelings. There are things I need to tell you about it, but it's all far too elaborate to tell right now…" he trailed off, and I had difficulty hearing his words.

He gently embraced me before he left, gripping me as if it would be the last time we saw each other. I hugged him tightly, hoping he would be safe.

"There's one last thing I forgot to tell you. You'll be safe under the fountain; Casimir doesn't even know it's there. My great-grandfather built it a long time ago, as a hiding place," he slid his arm through the bushes, "and I know you're not afraid; you never are." As he vanished, I caught a glimpse of his smile, and then I was alone again to face the night underground.

"But wait! What does the necklace do? Why do I need to protect it from Casimir?" I called, but he was already gone.

Before returning, I unclasped my fingers and saw why my father thought the necklace to be so…magical. Fastened by swirling wire to a chain was the most curious thing I'd ever seen. It was a silver circle, just big enough to fit around my wrist, and across the center were dozens of translucent strings woven together like a spider's web. At first glance, a sort of foggy light seemed to be radiating from the strings. As I stared at it, though, I realized the light was coming from the moon—but the strings had a luminous milky color to them. Carved elegantly around the silver circle were the words:

If you close your eyes and dream with me,
I will rid those things you wish not to see.

Could it be something to control my dreams? Thoroughly puzzled, I placed it around my neck, and a sensation passed through me so strong that I collapsed to my knees. At first it was weighted, heavy as a brick, but it was a peaceful weight, like carrying somebody I loved through a battlefield, hurting myself but knowing I would save them. Then as quickly as it came, the sensation disappeared, and I returned to my feet, feeling extremely happy and dismissing any questions that lingered in my mind because I knew I wouldn't be able to answer them.

I felt exhausted, but had to fight the desire to sleep because I wanted to avoid dreams.

Sliding the fountain back to reveal the hole, I paused before going under. Something felt odd; everything was so still. I flashed my head around to see a shadow break through the leaves.

I could smell him before I could see him: a scent of burnt things tumbled through the air, and I dove behind the fountain's shadow, not having enough time to cover the hole.

His hair was singed in places and soot was sprinkled over his clothes. As usual, he was the person I was least expecting to see.

"Where are you?" Casimir's voice angrily bellowed from somewhere in the distance.

Revelin stood before me, his blue eyes bulging with anticipation as he searched for a place to hide. He neared the hole in the earth, and with little hesitation climbed into it. My stomach dropped as I watched him, knowing he had found, and now occupied, my only hiding place.

Squatting uncomfortably over my toes for what seemed like half an hour, I waited for him to leave, but he didn't. Why was he running? Was he escaping from Casimir, or was Casimir calling for me? I listened for some sound below, but none came, so I crawled around the fountain and ducked my head to peek below.

Sure enough, he was sitting on the edge of the moss bed, cupping his chin in his hands and his elbows propped on his spread-apart knees. His eyes were unusually hollow, like an empty bowl, whereas they were normally profound. The light from the candle flickered feebly, dancing on the left side of his body.

I supposed he must have seen me, because he jumped slightly when he glanced in my direction, but I didn't move.

"Now who's doing the following?" He said, laughing a little as he motioned for me to come down. "How did you find me?"

Hesitantly, I descended the spiral stairs. I couldn't trust him yet. "I was here first," I answered, sounding like a child. I stayed a safe distance from him, "for…protection. I wasn't following."

He gave me his usual haughty smile, "You don't have to hide anything from me. I know why you're hiding here. It's because you have the Gift."

My hand reflexively shot forward and grabbed his arm firmly, as if he would run off at any second and tell Casimir. His arm was strong, but he didn't try to shake me off. Distress froze my blood and tingled through my fingers, making my bones feel brittle. I wanted to ask him how he found out, but all I said was:

"Does *he* know?"

Revelin winced and I let go of him, not detecting how tight my grip had been. His smile faded, "My dad? Yeah, he knows. Timoria spilled it to him when she found her sister dead, who'd been burned by the fire, back at the palace. She knew you caused it, and she got mad. I overheard her telling him, just after the melting stopped. My dad doesn't exactly believe her, but he suspects you. I knew what was going to happen after that; he'd make me help him catch you. I can't do it, though. I don't want the same things he does."

My eyes squinted as I watched his every movement, "But how did Timoria know?"

I also knew what Nico had meant; I knew what he was trying to explain when he said that Revelin wasn't bad. He meant that Casimir lived and thrived on power, doing whatever he could to get it, and Revelin thrived on something else, but I couldn't yet tell what it was.

"Timoria isn't all bad, you know. She's one of the few Deceivers who actually has a heart. But as we found out recently, she isn't good at keeping secrets. My mom, Lucetta, is friends with her. When my mom was our age, she was in love with your father. Yeah, don't tell me how creepy that is, I already know. My mom's known about the Gift for years, and she accidentally told Timoria about it once."

So it was Lucetta. She was the woman that my father loved.

The fact that my father once loved Revelin's mother bothered me a little, but the fact that Casimir might have known that I had the Gift bothered me even more.

"So now he's looking for me," I whispered somewhat to myself, realizing I might have to stay hidden for a long time now, the stinging remorse of my murders still lingering in my mind. My bare foot traced a crack on the moist rock floor.

"Yes, I think so, and me," he replied, "but can't you just get rid of them somehow? You know, make another fire or something like that? My father's told me a lot of stories about...your kind." The way he said it was aimed to sound like an insult, picking at me.

"It's not that easy," I answered, my voice steady, "Using the Gift can be extremely dangerous. Besides, you're a Deceiver, and Casimir's son. Just order them away from us; you should have enough power to do that."

He stood up and trudged to the spiral steps. Feeling that I could trust him enough for now, I left my defensive stance and took his place and sat on the moss bed.

"First of all, I'm barely a Deceiver, only part," his voice was firm but distant, "and I have no power over them; they all hate me anyway. Lilah, they're corrupt: they don't care about anything or anyone except for their damn leader." I could hear the anger in his voice now, at his people, and how he wished not to be one of them.

I was going to mention that he would be the future leader,

his father's heir, but I didn't desire to take it any further. That might then lead to his older sister Cyra's premature death, and how she was supposed to be the heir, but a horrible accident took her away at a young age. I always thought that was the main reason why everyone naturally disliked Revelin…because they wished he had died instead of his sister.

It felt strange, Revelin and I speaking to each other as if we had known each other for years, unafraid of one another. Revelin walked to the candle with wide strides. At first I thought he was doing it on purpose, stretching his legs maybe, but then I saw it was because of his height. He had lanky legs, but his long torso balanced his form. I thought for quite some time as he ceased his pointless pacing and sat beside me again.

"I'm actually glad, you know, that the palace burned. I didn't like being there; it was always so…dark," he paused for a while and glanced around the room. "How did this place even get here?" His blue eyes glowed in the dimness, as a ghost's might.

I told him about how my great-grandfather built it for a hiding place, and I was about to go into the history of the Gift, but not here…not to him. I hardly knew him; he could be deceiving me and I wouldn't even have time to comprehend it. His father was great at betraying people, why not Revelin?

He must have noticed the sudden suspicious look on my face because he then stopped asking questions.

"How do I know that you're not tricking me right now? You could go to Casimir whenever and tell him where I am," I said, my eyes narrowing questioningly.

He laughed, "You don't know whether or not I am. And judging by your personality, I probably won't be able to convince you to trust me. No matter what I say, you won't believe me. Am I right?"

"How could you judge my personality if you don't even *know* me?" I replied, but then cursed myself for being stubborn. I didn't want to fight; anger is a devastating thing.

His sly grin didn't recede as he sat there for a while, gazing at me, "I don't know what it is with you, but you're weird. I'm surprised you haven't *fallen in love* with me yet like the rest of them do."

I blinked in surprise.

I had heard from Ali how she, along with many other girls our age, swooned at the sight of Revelin, taken aback by his mysterious charm and looks. I *really* couldn't understand how that was possible. "Are you always this conceited?" I asked.

"Mostly just during the week," he answered, then laughed. "I'm messing with you; stop being so serious," he said, expecting me to fire back an insult.

"There's a gathering tomorrow," I said, changing the subject, "at the gate. I have to decide in the morning if I'll go." I then thought he would leave but he just sat there beside me inquisitively, with his eyebrows raised, amazed I hadn't tried to insult him.

Then I understood that he couldn't leave; where would he go?

I guessed his only real friend was Nico, but Casimir could have Deceivers waiting just outside, so he didn't want to risk it.

"It's okay," he said, standing up, "I'll sleep on the floor." He then spotted a large patch of moss in the corner of the room. "By the way, you have some dirt on your cheeks," he said finally before he lay down on the moss.

I was already settled into the small bed of moss, and I drew my hand up and swept my face, but it came back clean.

"They're freckles," I grunted back, for someone had said the same thing to me before.

"Oh," he replied, snickering, "sorry."

I rolled onto my side so my back was facing him. I wouldn't fall asleep. I would force myself not to. Dreams of any kind would not be productive especially since everyone was still recovering from the fire.

I couldn't, anyway, with those eyes penetrating me. Even behind his closed eyelids as he slept soundlessly, I could feel them burning into me. It seemed that was the only thing he had inherited from Casimir, the omniscient eyes, so blue.

What did it feel like, I wondered, to be lost? What would it be like to be confused, wandering in an unknown place with an unknown destination? I liked to think it would be wonderful, being unaware of what could happen within the next turn, not knowing what event could take place or what danger lurked ahead.

Somewhere between sleep and awake, so that I wouldn't

dream, I sat upright in the bed, startled, as I attempted to remember my destination. I found that when my eyes opened, everything was black as if they were still closed. My first reaction was that I was trapped in some nightmare world, or I dreamed about something horrible that became reality, until I heard a scraping sound not too far away that seemed to dig into my ears like a piercing shriek. I jumped from the bed onto the wet floor and slipped slightly.

"Who's there?" I nearly yelled, grasping my forehead as I felt dizzy from my sudden movement. My muscles ached from a sleepless night. I glanced down at my necklace, and it was…glowing? A single sunbeam wavered through a crack in the ceiling and seemed to be growing in size.

"Easy there, it's just me," Revelin's voice flowed down the now visible staircase as he laughed at my sleepy delusion. The room was illuminated brightly, the sun sparkling through the hole in the ceiling.

I glanced to where the candle had been, but all that remained was a melted mess. The glowing necklace must have been my imagination, because when I looked at it again, a plain webbed silver circle rested normally against my chest.

I caught my reflection in a flat puddle of water at my feet: I appeared tired, vicious, and wild, and felt annoyed at Revelin's sarcasm.

He sat on the top step, his plain, dark blue shirt absorbing the swirls of light, and I noticed something about him I hadn't seen before. I somewhat expected him to be wearing the metal belt as the townspeople had to, because he was so unlike a Deceiver, but there was no restriction on his waist. Still, he was thin and strong, but the lack of the belt made him seem so different.

His clothing, too, was unlike that which the town boys had to wear. The town boys wore plain white shirts and shorts in the warm weather, and his clothing was dark and more difficult to see in the night.

The smile on his lips faded as he became aware of my lingering gaze where his belt should be. Descending the stairs, he came to a stop in front of me, a little too close for my liking, and I took a step back for space. He didn't move, but those omniscient eyes were inescapable, imprisoning me no matter where I ran.

"Look, I know how you feel. The belts weren't my idea, so don't look at me like I'm responsible. I'm nothing like my father," he said, his voice containing that hint of the Deceivers' honey-like quality, drawing flies into a trap.

But there was still something unreliable about him. "I'm glad you're nothing like your father, but then maybe you could have at least told him how unnecessary the belts and his stalking Deceivers are, no?" This bickering was pointless, but for some reason unavoidable.

In reply, Revelin stepped closer to me again, until we were just a foot apart, and my back was nearly pressed against the cold rock wall opposite the staircase. I was about to speak when he reached his hands forward and clasped them around my belt.

Within seconds, he twisted the metal as if it were rubber

and it snapped, clattering to the floor around my feet. I was amazed because I thought the metal was thick, but maybe it was more flexible than I thought.

"Better?" He cracked a pearly grin, but then we were silent. We stood motionless for a minute, neither of us speaking, staring at one another, realizing he just broke his father's own rule.

I wanted to say something, but it seemed whatever needed to be said was pointless.

My fingers instinctively glided across my chest, relieved when I felt the necklace still there. For some reason, I kept thinking he wanted to steal it from me. Unnoticeably, I tucked it into my tunic so it was hidden from view. I felt as if it would be the only part of my father I would be seeing again soon.

Revelin's face was inches from my own. His eyes glazed over as they glanced at my lips and he began leaning forward, grinning lazily. My chest shriveled. His hot breath fanned across my cheeks.

Before anything further could happen on a personal level, I swerved around him and headed for the stairs, "We need to go to that gathering whether we want to or not. If he notices that I'm not present, he'll know for sure that I have the Gift."

Revelin turned to face me and nodded, disappointment just barely detectable in his eyes, "It's still early morning; nobody'll be awake yet. Let's go to Nico's house first; we have to disguise ourselves so we'll be unrecognizable."

At the mention of changing clothes, I looked down to find myself wet and grimy, my tunic-dress filthy and my hair, cascading down to the middle of my back, was matted and muddy. It was strange not having the belt restricting me, the cloth of the garment hung loosely around my waist. I immediately agreed with him, and we climbed the stairs into the early morning sun.

6 Into The Silver Hand

The grass still felt dewy underneath my feet as I stepped onto it, the soft blades tickling my ankles, and the day was sultry and sluggish. The area was clear of any Deceivers, clear of any life, in fact: I didn't hear a single bird chirp or the faint hum of insect wings. Revelin came up from the hole behind me, easily moving the stone to conceal it again. We neared the line of bushes soundlessly, peering through a few of the branches.

"We have to go along the alleys; anywhere else will be too open and our footsteps will be easily heard," I whispered to him, expecting him not to know anything about the town and feeling good that I knew something that he didn't.

"Whatever you say," he replied with a hint of sarcasm and boldness.

I turned my head to look at him, my face still, "Please, if you want to lead, feel free."

He coughed uncomfortably and shifted his weight from one foot to the other. "No…uh, sorry, continue." I should have felt satisfied, but I was indifferent, my thoughts wandering to Casimir's gathering as I stepped through the bushes to get to the street.

Revelin was right on my tail as I flew through the alleys, but for some reason he seemed a million miles away, and I repeatedly checked behind me to make sure he was still there.

Perhaps I just didn't want him to run off and tell Casimir. But there was another reason too…and after some thought I found what it was: he was too unpredictable. I didn't understand him, which was why I didn't trust him. People like Andrew and Ali were usually predictable, kindhearted, and didn't keep secrets, and I trusted them with my life.

The streets were empty and not a soul was in sight, which made the short trip to Nico's house feel longer than it was. The warm sun brilliantly reflected off the white homes, and Revelin shielded his eyes and I squinted as it continued to rise. Just as we reached Nico's front steps, people began to awaken and come outside. I lifted my fist to knock on his front door but Revelin, noticing the townspeople coming out, moved around me and pushed the door open without hesitation, letting himself inside.

Thereby confirming my assumption of his unpredictable nature, I entered after him, shutting the door behind me. We came into a scene of Nico's sitting at his kitchen table eating breakfast, his hair in a wild mess on his head and his mother fighting him with grease-smothered hands to try to fix it.

"Mom, *stop*," he complained as he dodged her hands, then

looked at us with a startled expression, as if he had just seen a ghost. His mother wailed dramatically, her arms flailing in the air, flinging the grease across the room.

"Robbers! Help!" she cried, her cheeks flushing so red with surprise that they almost matched the color of her red-gold hair. I thought Nico would have tried to calm her, but even I knew she was unreachable in that state. Revelin attempted to explain, but she was blinded by her hysteria and ignored him, and her shrieks vibrated through the house until Nico's father groggily stumbled out of the bedroom and into the kitchen.

"Regina," he mumbled, rubbing his weary eyes and watching as she scrambled, screaming, around the room. She continued, ignoring him, and he steadied himself to say loudly, "*Regina Aljoy*! Get a hold on yourself; look who it is." He pointed a chubby finger in my direction and a smile spread across his kind face, his eyes twinkling.

Regina paused in her screeching to glance at me, and flashed a feeble grin, but continued to cry, allowing Nico's father to wrap her in a hug. It was a strange sight, Regina's paper-thin stringy body being swallowed by his large physique. I nearly suffocated myself trying to contain my laughter at her. It was a challenge every time I was near her, but I managed it.

Nico, however, was less controlled and burst into laughter as Mrs. Aljoy glared at him through her tears. But soon enough, he had her giggling, because his laugh was *dead* contagious. I exchanged a glance with him, and it felt unfamiliar, almost as if I didn't know him, because the last time we were together I found a whole different side to him.

As the ruckus calmed, Mr. Aljoy released Regina and drew Revelin and me into a large hug. "Lilah, Revelin, it's great to see you two. What brings you here so early?"

"Yeah, way to ruin my beauty treatment," Nico mumbled. But Mr. Aljoy's expression was serious; my father had probably told him something about the situation with the Gift and Casimir's knowledge.

"We have to disguise ourselves for the gathering," Revelin replied, not indicating anything else.

"Your house was the farthest we could get before people started waking up, so we were hoping we could get ready here. My father probably already told you how Casimir possibly knows about the Gift," I added, not sounding as demanding as Revelin had implied. After hearing myself say it, I realized just how unwise it would be for me to wander right into Casimir's arms.

Mr. Aljoy nodded, but before he could answer, Regina stepped in front of him and grabbed my shoulders, a nauseatingly excited grin on her lips, "Of course sweetie, let me help you." She giddily led me back into her room but turned to add, "Oh and Nico, give Revelin some clothes, will you?"

She dragged me into her and Mr. Aljoy's drab bedroom and ordered me to take a shower, which I did with some objection because I disliked following orders; but I finally gave in because Regina accused me of being a 'stubborn mess' and I wanted to shower anyway. The fresh, cool water felt soothing and I scrubbed myself clean of the grime, and washed my hair. Regina had awful soaps that smelled of dead things, but I used them anyway, and walked out in my towel to find her fussing over two tunic dresses of the same color.

"Maroon or burgundy?" She asked herself, holding one in each hand and examining them closely.

"White will be fine," I said loudly, thinking she wouldn't be able to hear me over her intense concentration, "I want to be disguised, right? Nearly everyone wears white."

"Oh yes! Of course, that's genius," she exclaimed, tossing the tunics into a large pile of others consisting of every color in the world. I suppressed an eye-roll as she pulled a flawless white one out of a closet and handed it to me, the soft fabric seeming to float between my fingers because it was so light.

She handed me some fresh undergarments and I retreated to the bathroom, dressed, and felt the light fabric of the tunic drift down around my body. I looked briefly in the mirror at the clothing, feeling irritated that my appearance was the same as every other girl's, which was why I usually preferred colored things instead of white. I took the webbed silver necklace out of my pile of dirty clothes on the floor and placed it around my neck, tucking it out of view again.

When I returned to the bedroom, I found another unpleasant surprise. Regina was holding a pair of small, tight shoes in her hands and staring at me expectantly. I wanted to refuse, but I knew it had to be done, and I wiggled my free toes one last time through the scraggly, plain gray carpet.

As I tugged the shoes onto my feet, surprised they were the right size because my feet were somewhat smaller than hers, I glanced up at Regina, noticing her pink tunic, excessive jewelry, and straight hair. I could imagine her wearing makeup, if we had ever seen it before. The only way I knew it existed was that on rare occasions Casimir would bring in a few things from the World Beyond the Walls besides food and necessities to help satisfy his wife, but they never worked. Secretly, she would show them to the curious children in town, and once she showed us the thing called 'makeup.'

Regina's eyes flashed to where my belt used to be, and she looked suspicious, but waved it away and unclasped her own.

"Here, use mine," she said, handing it to me, but I felt hesitant. "It's only for today; you can give it back to me after the gathering."

I fastened the cold metal band around my waist, "But won't they notice you?"   She grinned as she went to her closet and drew out a shiny golden sash, tying it securely where the belt should be.

"I know, I know. I'm just brilliant, don't you think? They won't even be able to tell the difference," she giggled, bouncing on the balls of her feet as an excited child might. The Deceivers were blind, so they would feel each townsperson's waist to make sure the belts were being worn, and they would surely detect the falsity in Regina's, but they rarely checked anyway. I nodded and smiled to give her the satisfaction, because I knew that any other response would cause her to cry, and after all she *was* helping me.

"This should be perfect, but I think I should cover my face more, because I'm too visible," I told her as she grabbed a brown cloak from the pile of clothes. After placing it around me, she put the hood over my head, and finally I felt as if I would be unrecognizable. Glancing out the window, I saw that the sun was creeping higher and the gathering would begin in no more than an hour.

"Thank you, Regina, I couldn't have done it without you," I said as we neared the bedroom door. I turned the knob to open it, but before I did, she said something that made me stop.

"It's obvious, if you weren't aware," she whispered quietly, standing right behind me. I turned my head to face her, my mind reeling with what she could mean.

"What is?" I asked, trying not to sound too confused.

She took no extra time to answer, overjoyed that she knew something I was interested in and unaware of, "That somebody has feelings for you. You know who I mean."

She expected me to answer, but I stood there, baffled, the tight shoes pinching my feet and my still-wet hair soaking my garments. I wanted to go out to get some food, then dry in the sun, but her comment made me curious, which would mean I would stay until I figured it out. "No, I don't know who you mean."

"Lilah, it's my son, Nico," Regina spat out, gawking at me as if I were the most unintelligent person that ever lived, "I can see the way he looks at you. All these years, and you've never realized? And you'd better stay away from him; he's not old enough for those kinds of feelings yet. If I see you anywhere too near him, I'll be sure to take action. Remember, the Deceivers punish young love because it leads to rebellion."

At first, no thoughts entered my mind. Then I felt uncomfortable, nauseated even, wanting to get out and not speak to Regina anymore.

"You can think whatever you want, but I know he *doesn't* feel that way. He never has, and he never will. We—we just really care for each other, that's all. And please believe me, I don't have those feelings for him."

My face flushed like fire as I calmly but swiftly swung open the door and tried to remain steady as I passed a laughing Nico and Mr. Aljoy in the kitchen, talking about something funny. Nico immediately noticed my attitude as I walked by and went to sit on the front step outside in the sun.

Townspeople wandered around, preparing for the gathering, but no Deceivers were in sight so I carelessly pulled off the hood and let the sun dry my hair. I stared down at a tuft of grass growing from the stone step and allowed the breeze to soothe my troubled mind.

Regina was wrong, I was sure of it. I knew Nico well, and he never had feelings for me. He was really caring and maybe that came off as love, but it just couldn't be. Kind, strong-hearted Nico,

I loved him, but not like that.

I sat there for an hour, finally dry, watching as a few children solemnly trudged by on their way to the gathering in front of the Shadow Kingdom. Normally, in that land beyond the walls, I liked to imagine children would be happier and more free, and I hoped someday I could see it.

Just as I was about to stand and go inside to eat before we departed, the front door opened and Nico came out and sat beside me. He was dressed in the usual white shirt and shorts, but he hadn't allowed his mother to fix his hair, so it spiked out wildly. He looked worried, or confused, but I couldn't tell which. I could usually decipher others' emotions, but it was difficult with Nico.

He wouldn't look at me, only gaze at the passing townspeople, his hands tightly gripping the stone step, and the sun illuminated his hair until it matched the color of his metal belt. He didn't utter a word, but his mouth was ajar as if he wanted to say something.

"It'll be fine, Nico, they won't recognize me," I said, readjusting the hood again so that only my face was visible. "They're blind, remember?" I laughed a little, which made him less tense. I placed my hand on top of his, and his grip softened. I didn't care what Regina said, I cared for him, and I wouldn't let her accusation of love get in the way of that.

He returned the laugh, but quietly, in case a Deceiver was near. "You're not afraid of *anything*, are you?" Then he stiffened again. "Why are you going, if it would be safer to stay under the fountain? Your father told us how you would be living there for a while, but I didn't know...*Revelin* would be living with you." I could sense anger in his voice at the last words, but I tried to ignore it.

"I have to go because if I don't, the Deceivers will notice my absence and *know* that I'm the one with the Gift," I answered, "and Revelin isn't living with me; he needs a place to hide because his father wants to use him against me." I paused, running my idle right hand along the cracked paint of the railing beside me as I felt a few pieces chip off and crumble against my fingers, "And yes, of course I'm afraid of some things."

Nico nodded, but he still seemed uncomfortable with the whole thing, and he gazed at me for a long time as if it were the last time he would see me. I didn't return the gaze, not because I was afraid, but because I felt it would turn into something more.

"Then what *are* you afraid of?" He finally asked.

I had to think for a minute, wondering if I should reveal my fears to him. Perhaps I would say something simple and typical so that he wouldn't ask too many questions. "That someone I love will die."

I expected him to be like everyone else and say 'that wouldn't matter, because you could just bring them back to life by dreaming about them,' but he didn't. The truth was, that if I did get a chance to bring someone back to life, I don't think I would. Bringing a soul back to a body just didn't seem right. It's like caging a bird after it was just set free.

His hand beneath mine had been idle, but then he gently

moved it so that we were clasping each other's. "That's not going to happen anytime soon," he reassured me, and I smiled at him.

Within a minute, the front door swung open and Revelin walked out, also dressed in the usual white clothes and a brown hood, and he even had Mr. Aljoy's metal belt around his waist. The belt looked so out of place and droopy because he was slender and Mr. Aljoy was so great.

He stood in the doorway, gnawing on a biscuit with his usual lazy expression, but it faded when he saw my hand placed on Nico's and us sitting close together. He looked annoyed, and he tried to hide it, but it was unmistakable.

"When you lovebirds are done, we have to leave." Within seconds he tossed me a large, fresh biscuit, turned, and went back inside. "O Romeo, Romeo! Wherefore art the cow Romeo?" He chuckled mockingly as he slammed the door, and I heard Regina squeak from inside.

"It's *wherefore art thou*!" I corrected.

"Whatever," he grunted from inside.

I removed my hand from Nico's and caught the food, feeling angry. "*What is it* with them today? They make accusations at the *slightest* gesture." I hungrily ate the bread while confusion spread on Nico's face.

"*Them*? Who's *them*?" He asked. Suddenly, I realized I gave away that somebody else had said we had feelings for each other, but I wasn't going to tell him about Regina.

"No, I meant Revelin. I don't understand why he had to say

that," I replied, attempting to cover up. Lying, it was one of the things I *hated* most in the entire world. Nico wasn't convinced, but he let it pass because he was just as uncomfortable with the subject as I was.

As I finished the food, I wiped my hands free of crumbs on the tunic and let a smile flicker on my lips as a fresh breeze thick with the aroma of flowers wafted to my nose.

"Lilah," Nico began, taking a deep breath, slightly puffing out his cheeks, and then gently releasing it as he always did when he was about to say something profound, "I need to know something, please."

"Nico, don't," I said. I didn't want him to affect our friendship, but his tawny eyes were fiery with youthful determination. I didn't want him to mention the feelings that Regina had told me about.

The number of people on the streets began to decrease, so to change the subject, I decided we had to leave. Nico and I went into the house once more to find the three of them still eating at the table. I felt awed to see that Revelin ate just as much as Mr. Aljoy, but then remembered he grew up in the palace where food was always abundant.

Regina frowned and narrowed her eyes at me, indicating she thought that Nico and I had been kissing or something, so I ignored her. Revelin didn't even glance at us, but attempted to appear careless as he ate his food. Nico's family hardly ever got this much food because Casimir thought Mr. Aljoy overate, and there was

Revelin, shamelessly swallowing as much as he could, and Nico's passive family didn't say a word.

"Revelin," I said, walking over and pulling the fork from his hand, "I think that's enough." At first he looked impressed that I would do such a thing, but then noticed how little the others were eating, and genuinely apologized to them.

Mr. Aljoy stood and peered out the window: "Quickly, we have to go, the town is nearly empty. If we're late, the Deceivers will surely notice us." The others stood and we grouped in a circle before going outside. "We'll have to split up; Casimir expects Lilah to be with either her family, Ali, or us. Nico and Regina, come with me, and Mr. Ridger you stay with Lilah."

Revelin, feeling proud once again, laughed a little, "I don't take orders from anyone." My skin crawled with disappointment at him as Mr. Aljoy looked offended but didn't reply.

"Then *leave*, Revelin. We don't need you. You're the one that came to me for a place to hide, remember?" My voice was slightly sweet, which only made him wince even more.

He was quiet then, giving me a cold scowl, but not objecting to the plans. As Mr. Aljoy continued, his round cheeks bounced with each word. We were to separate, listen to Casimir's speech, then meet back at the house. As we filed out of the house and onto the street, Nico didn't leave my side. A few times I felt his shoulder brush mine because he was so close, and Revelin was on my other side, not too far away. Nico's parents were ahead of us, and Regina turned her head and silently motioned Nico to come up to them.

He gave me a final half-smile, and then looked at Revelin, "Take care of her, and be alert." I knew Revelin would have objected and said he didn't take orders, but Nico was his friend, so he only nodded.

As Nico darted ahead to get to his parents, I noticed the sun was hot and high in the sky, and the stone road seemed endless. Revelin was right beside me, keeping a watchful eye on the street, and pulling his own hood over his head. A few townspeople passed us, hurrying their children along, so we quickened our pace. Nico's family was out of sight, meshed into the crowd of people who were nearly running to get to the gathering.

As we were about a minute away from the Shadow Kingdom, Revelin finally spoke. I thought he was going to be angry at me, or annoyed, but he merely said, "It's going to be strange, seeing that place destroyed. All of it melted. I'm glad though; I hated it there." I realized that he was secretly thanking me, happy that my fire had caused the place to be demolished.

I wanted to answer, but before I could, we arrived at the boundary between the town and the Shadow Kingdom. Some way ahead, I could see the large crowd of townspeople and Deceivers grouped around the glowing blue lamppost, which had survived the fire. Casimir wasn't yet in view, but I could see a large, metal block with stairs that leading to it, in the center of the crowd. This was where he would stand. The sunlight reflected off the metal, making it look white.

I expected to see remains of the melted palace, but it was already being rebuilt and was almost halfway finished. There were a few blackened and melted heaps of metal off to the side, but the Deceivers were repairing at breakneck speed.

There were still a few families arriving around us, and relaxing because weren't that late, we paused at the border. Simultaneously, Revelin and I looked at each other, knowing that we were walking right into the enemy's grasp.

7 The Capture Of The Innocent

We made a quiet agreement that we would not leave each other's side, and without hesitation, Revelin reached over and grabbed my right hand. Normally I would have objected, but he needed something to hold on to.

Tugging on the hoods to further conceal our faces, we crossed onto the silver floor. I didn't like the feeling of the ground beneath my bare feet because it was hot and slippery, so I was thankful to be wearing shoes. The same thought seemed to be passing through Revelin's mind as he glared briefly at the metal.

Usually one might expect a crowd to be noisy or wild, but this crowd was so silent I could almost hear my own heart beating. The people were still as Deceivers wandered around, their hoods covering their faces as the sun was so bright.

Revelin and I slid into the multitude, not speaking a word, and not lifting our heads from their bowed positions. I focused on the people's feet around me, because the ground was not trustworthy. It was so flawless, it could lead anywhere and I wouldn't notice.

I caught the eye of a nearby Deceiver, and I could tell that they were overly vigilant, and that they were looking for me. Revelin's grip was so tight it caused my knuckles to turn white, but I hardly noticed. A sidelong glance at him told me that even he was uneasy.

The few hushed voices around us immediately grew silent and I could hear the distinct sound of Casimir's heavy footsteps pounding the stairs that led to the tall, metal block. Each step seemed to vibrate through the crowd, causing the people to become so quiet that we might as well have been standing in a graveyard.

Revelin's breath caught in his throat as his father stepped onto the platform, his blinding white cloak fluttering in the soupy wind. He appeared infuriated and thinner than usual, so thin that I could see his ribs protruding, and his pale arms trembled. Droopy skin sagged beneath his eyes and his lips were so colorless and cracked they could have been those of a corpse. His lifeless eyes were still and when he yelled so that the crowd could hear, his voice was weak and quivering.

"Welcome," he began, his words echoing through the air, "my precious people."

I had been expecting that he would say that, as he always did, but what interested me was that his attitude was not sarcastic and vulgar as usual; it was almost forced and fearful.

The crowd erupted into neat, hasty applause that caused Revelin to cringe with disgust. I felt his warm hand sweating and his muscles tensing, as if he would run off at any second and attack somebody. The will to fight was evident in his expressive movements. A Deceiver passed us and caught my eye, and I prayed he wasn't the kind that could see. He continued without hesitation, however, and Casimir began speaking again.

"I have called you here today because a miracle has happened," he announced, beaming.

Before another word was spoken, I heard a familiar shriek. My eyes darted up immediately, searching the crowd, only to land upon a sight that made my heart freeze. Near the podium where Casimir stood, a few Deceivers seized someone and dragged them onto the metal block for the multitude to see. Then another person followed, then another. I knew them well, but I didn't allow my mind to think about it, because chaos would break loose.

All three of them were then handcuffed with glistening golden rings. The smallest of them took quivering, short breaths that screamed with fear and the others' jaws were rigid. Revelin's grip rose from my hand onto my wrist, restraining me instead of protecting me.

One of them, I wouldn't allow myself to tell which, released a half-hearted wail. The crowd around me was stiff, knowing any movement would be dangerous, and my breathing halted as I waited for Casimir's next words.

"As you can see, the people standing behind me are Aaron, Jane, and Andrew Keeper. Fifteen years ago, the Gift was passed from Aaron onto his first child." As Casimir spoke, my very limbs were shaking with each word, but Revelin's grip was steady, unbreakable. "For hundreds of years, my ancestors have sought to find that person, and now I have. I know you are out there, Lilah." His cold eyes raked through the crowd as if he could see. The crowd should have gasped, but they remained silent, and I knew I could trust them to help me.

I forced myself to remain still as I caught my father's eye, and he slightly shook his head as if telling me not to reveal myself. I should have been frightened, but I felt frustration, and wondered how I could escape.

"If you don't show yourself, your family will be dead by tonight." He said it so casually he could have been talking about the weather. But he was serious. I had been expecting his threat, for I had heard similar ones before, but when he actually spoke it, I jumped with astonishment.

I could no longer stand it; my insides were wrenching, and so I suddenly lifted my head and flailed my free arm, and attempted to lunge into the crowd closer to Casimir. I cursed myself for impulsiveness, but the multitude must have seen me, for as soon as I began moving, they too went into fits of yelling and running around so as to conceal me. I wanted them to stop so I could show myself and save my family, even if it would mean Casimir would use me for his evil purposes. Revelin was planted to the ground: I couldn't yank free of his grip, and Deceivers madly charged the townspeople.

Somehow, I managed to scream, "Let go!" But Revelin was linked to me with an indestructible bond, and when I turned to glance at him, his face was stern. Chaos had broken loose; Casimir had stepped down from the podium and was searching the crowd for me, as every Deceiver did the same.

"We need to go!" Revelin shouted over the riot of the people. "Trust me, they won't hurt your family!"

As soon as he spoke he knew that he had made a mistake. My jaw clenched at his words, and he knew that I didn't trust him. I struggled and cried, trying to get the Deceivers' attention, but none came near me. Within seconds, Revelin deftly swooped down and lifted me, so one arm was underneath my back and the other under my knees. The crowd was hostile, noticing as my hood fell back to reveal my face. I saw children screaming around me, drawing attention to themselves, and I pounded Revelin's back with my fist, but he remained calm as he quickly maneuvered around the crowd towards the town.

I kicked and wailed, attempting to get loose, and I knew it was useless, but I wanted my family back. Multiple times Deceivers crossed our path; one swung his fist, but we ducked, and then they moved on because they were too occupied with the townspeople to be able to tell what was happening.

I was breathing quickly, my throat swelled with the syrupy air, and my eyes darted to a face I knew well. Nico pushed through the people, trying to get to us, and his expression was panicky. I reached my hand as far toward him as I could, willing him to come with more haste, but it wasn't until his fingertips touched mine that I saw the horde of Deceivers pulling him back. One ducked low and clasped cuffs around his ankles, and another yanked back on his hair, but I grabbed his wrist.

Revelin was thrown backward and nearly slipped on the metallic ground as the Deceivers pulled the three of us into the crowd. He glanced behind him momentarily and I could sense his pity as he observed Nico. Nonetheless, he begged me to let go, saying I only made things worse, but I couldn't avoid Nico's pleading stare. A particularly alert Deceiver grabbed my wrist and smirked maniacally, so I angrily whipped my arm back and Revelin surged forward in a straining jog.

Each of Revelin's steps vibrated through my body and I felt motionless. I felt as if I was trapped beside Nico, aware of each cold hand hitting him until he was unconscious. He disappeared into the crowd which was filing out, dashing toward the town and just yards behind us.

I watched as Andrew was carried off the podium and toward the palace. Numbness overcame me and the desire to help him burned me like the sun above. As we crossed the border, the people slowed but Revelin maintained a steady pace, jogging through the streets.

"Put me down…Revelin," I demanded. He continued without stopping, breathing deeply, the wind whipping back his hood and hair to reveal his face. I felt lightheaded with anger, my eyes catching each of the townspeople's faces as they glanced quickly at me and then retreated to their homes. I tried to smile to show my gratitude, but I couldn't bring forth enough joy. The number of people decreased as we neared the fountain.

"It's not safe yet," Revelin panted. "They'll invade the town until they find us. I promise, your family's safe, I'll explain when…" his voice caught when a quiet, sweet voice pervaded the air.

"Revelin," it cried, almost pleadingly, sounding incredibly like Lucetta's.

I turned my head to see Timoria running toward us, just a little behind. She must have heard his voice, because she had us clearly picked out from the other townspeople. Revelin's eyes instantly widened and I could sense his muddled emotion; it was almost tangible: he was deciding whether to turn or continue running. She grinned mischievously at me, and I knew she was attempting to deceive Revelin.

"No, Revelin! It's Timoria: she's trying to deceive you," I warned him as Timoria emitted a cry of pain. Her shriek reached my ears like poisoned honey, and for a second I almost believed she was actually Lucetta in need of help. He stared searchingly at me as he slowed slightly. Timoria's trick was too convincing. In the moment he whipped his head around to look at her, she sprang forward and wrapped her hands around my neck like a noose.

Revelin was jerked to a halt, and my hands reflexively lifted and tried to pry Timoria's fingers away. She laughed sadistically and her bush of hair bounced with each movement. Swiftly, Revelin's foot kicked back into Timoria's stomach and she crumpled onto the street, clutching her middle and shrieking.

Revelin clenched his jaw in frustration as we flew away from the scene and into the deserted town. I kept my gaze on Timoria as the view of her cringed body on the street drifted farther away.

The townspeople were no longer visible and were far behind, still caught in the crowd, and Revelin's footsteps were the only ones audible for what seemed like miles. He slowed his pace to a slow jog as we felt we were alone.

"Why would you pick me up? That is by far the worst decision you could have made. MY FAMILY IS BACK THERE," I breathed. I wanted more than anything for him to put me down. I was more than capable of walking, but I knew he wouldn't because his stubbornness would not allow it.

He maintained his jog and huffed between breaths, "I—do—what—I—want." He hoisted me higher into his arms as I flopped furiously like a caged bird. "And also, I—saved—your—life." How could he keep his poise after such an event?

"You said that your father won't harm my family and friends, but I don't believe you. Why would he keep them alive?" I asked, my breath caught in my throat.

He sighed and his jaw muscles tensed as he regained his breath, "Calm down. He's done this same thing before when he thought a different person had the Gift. He didn't kill the family until he captured the person he suspected and found out that they didn't have it. He only ever acts out of anger. He won't harm your family until you turn yourself in…they're the bait, and you're the prized fish."

His words allowed me to relax enough that I stopped trying to free myself from his grasp. Casimir really was talented at deceiving people, but for now, my family was safe.

"And why would you want to save me?" I asked, wondering why he would choose to protect me. Sometimes I needed to ask irrelevant questions to distract my mind from worry.

"Because I actually have a heart, to your surprise. If you think it's because I like you, then you're wrong. You know, I actually thought you might have been an interesting person before I knew you. But now that I do, I feel exactly the opposite," he answered.

"The way that I look at it, you stopped me from saving my family. And you're bothered because I don't care to satisfy you. Everyone's blind to the fact that you have something rotten buried just beneath the surface," I said.

"Oh, so you like what's on the surface?" he said smugly and raised his eyebrows so that they disappeared into his wavy bangs. "Now stop asking questions," he panted.

I closed my eyes and sighed with disappointment, "You, Revelin, are deficient…and your pride is impossible."

"*My* pride?" He spat, chuckling once more, "and how am I *deficient*?"

The air was still before I replied, opening my eyes and gazing at the line of houses. "You're just a boy."

Parting his lips to reply, he suddenly pressed them together in a loss for words as he huffed a frustrated breath. His eyebrows were knitted together as a puzzled look crossed his face.

We dropped the conversation, and all was quiet as the afternoon sun tainted the rows of suburban houses a pale orange, and danced on our skin. I suppressed tears, even though I was internally boiling at the death threat to my family.

I closed my eyes and pictured the scene again. The way back to the fountain would be long, and the Deceivers would be flooding this part of town soon, but I comforted myself with thinking they were still dealing with the townspeople back at the palace.

"Will you put me down now?" I asked, my hand balling into a fist briefly and then releasing as I felt irritated. I couldn't understand how he had enough endurance to keep up a jog for so long.

"I can't trust you to stay with me; I know you'll run back to the palace for your family," he answered.

I felt defeated because he was right; I would just go back. "This needs to end; we have to find a way to trust each other, somehow. We can't just continue not knowing…not knowing if one of us will betray the other."

"Alright, I agree. How should we begin?" he said.

"Well, first, you have to be less unpredictable," I suggested as he glanced at me disapprovingly.

"I didn't realize I was being unpredictable, but I'll try to be… simpler, if that's what you're asking. And you have to be less impulsive; I'm never expecting what you'll do next and you always tend to get yourself into trouble," he said, his arms closing around me more tightly as, I assumed, he felt that I was going to begin struggling again.

"It's a deal," I replied, sighing deeply. We passed house after house, each white wall whispering me a story, all appearing the same on the outside, but those living within holding a unique tale itching to be told; but seeming unimportant by the holders who have forgotten its meaning. Every roof was the same gray, every door an identical brown, and they stretched on forever.

After nearly ten minutes, I saw the green bushes flutter into view in the distance, and Revelin stopped in his steady tracks. He gracefully placed me onto the ground as if he had done it a hundred times before.

"I'll let you walk from here, but you still have to hold my hand," he ordered, extending his hand to me as I glared.

"I thought we were going to practice trusting each other. I won't run back, I promise," I said as I ripped off my painful shoes.

"Alright, I'll try to believe you," he said.

As we swiftly treaded to the bushes which were still quite far away, I whipped my head around only to see the tendril of a shadow disappear behind a house. I grabbed Revelin's firm shoulder and whispered into his ear, "We have a follower."

He immediately turned and faced the empty street behind us, his hands rolling into fists. Veins throbbed in his arms and his jaw clenched.

"Show yourself, Timoria," he shouted. His voice contained the hint of Deceiver honey, making it so that even I had the desire to obey.

"Your directness will only cause conflict," I hissed, urging him to hide with me behind one of the white porches, but he would not be persuaded.

The evening sky threatened to turn into night within a few hours, faint stars taunting me as they became clearer, but the sun remained visible. My face flushed with anticipation as the shadow reappeared, casting darkness onto the street. Revelin prepared himself to pounce, when a small, fragile face surrounded by blonde curls innocently crept into view. She giggled mockingly while pointing at Revelin. "He thought I was a Deceiver!" She was just a child, but some children are the wittiest things.

Instantly I recognized her, and a sigh of relief enveloped my body. I caught a brief embarrassed glower from Revelin before she ceased her laughing and glanced nervously along the street.

She stepped out and scampered toward us, the previous joy drained from her pretty face and replaced by misery which sputtered out with each delicate movement. Her little hands were folded awkwardly behind her back as she stared in alarm at Revelin, realizing she had insulted Casimir's son.

"Tara," I whispered, recognizing we were an easy target for Deceivers, "what are you doing here? Why aren't you with Ali?"

As soon as I asked, I knew the answer, and Tara sniffled back a tear. Shifting uncomfortably from foot to foot, she switched her gaze from Revelin to me, "Casimir took Ali and the rest of my family, and Nico's family too. Ali knew we would be taken as prisoners, and she told me to escape before the Deceivers grabbed me. I begged her to come too, but she said that the Deceivers would be looking for her. I ran away just in time, and before she was taken, she told me to tell you not to rescue them and to escape over the walls. She said that the Gift is more important than anything else."

I kneeled and clutched Tara into a comforting hug as she broke into teary whimpers, "It's alright, we'll find a way to get them out, I promise. You'll be okay, Tara."

"Lilah, we have to leave," Revelin said while glancing around. "The Deceivers could be here any minute."

I nodded, kissed the top of Tara's head, and stood, "Tara, come stay with us; you need a place to hide."

She shook her head, yellow curls bouncing wildly, "No, it's okay. I'm staying with my aunt and uncle." Revelin tapped his foot impatiently and with a final weak smile Tara scampered down the road from where she came and vanished into an alley.

I rested my face in my hands for a moment as we continued to the bushes, and Revelin's eyes were shadowy with vigilance. Ali, Nico, and my family were sacrificing their lives for me, and when I should feel grateful I couldn't help but feel furious. Kind, innocent people who deserved nothing but happiness and freedom were probably locked in a cell deep below the palace, while I walked without restraint to hide myself from danger. How selfish I had become! What a coward I had become!

Revelin remained close to me, just inches to my right side, his chin slightly raised in a condescending manner. The adrenaline remained in his body, for he walked with a forceful, unsteady pace.

The sun began to sink behind the wall and a mysterious moon crawled into the sky behind me, and I wondered if a moon could ever be fuller. It lingered there like an unwanted guest—or like Revelin, I suppose, both of them being demeaning and undesired.

Revelin glanced at me from the corner of his eye, "Let me guess, you're thinking about how much you wish I weren't here right now."

"Yes…" I began accidentally but then clenched my teeth together as my eyes widened, "I mean no, I-I wasn't, why would you think…"

"I could tell by the way you were scowling at me," he interrupted, nonchalantly shoving his hands into his pockets and setting his shoulders back, "But it's alright; you're no more pleasant to be around."

The bushes were no more than a minute away but it felt like miles. My final ounce of tolerance, which had been hanging by a thread, snapped at his words. I stepped in front of him so that he was forced to stop and face me, but not a hint of care or fear was present in his mysterious eyes.

"I've had enough, Revelin," words tumbled off my tongue, quiet and tight with anger, "I've been kind enough to share my hiding place with you, and if all you can repay me with is carelessness and constant fighting, then I want you to leave. Go home to you father."

He chuckled and stepped closer so that our faces were merely inches apart. "*Your* hiding place? Let me explain something, Lilah," he moved his head so that his lips were beside my ear and his next words came with an icy breath that caused me to shudder, "I *own* you." He drew his head back with a smirk and waited for a reply.

"The only thing you *own* is a head full of self-induced lies," I said calmly.

His grin twitched and receded, "I'm one of the most important people in this place, and I own almost everything; tell me how that's a lie." Slight annoyance had become evident in his features though he tried to conceal it.

"Don't be so modest," I said, which made his cheeks pink. I turned to keep walking, only to have him trailing on my heels.

"You're just an ordinary person, and I'm Casimir's son. Yet you act like you have power over me." He fumed, quietly keeping up with my quick pace.

I didn't reply as we reached the bushes. I parted them with my arm and slid through, followed by his Highness.

We faced each other once fully concealed, the mixed sunlight and moonlight slithering like snakes through the grass, and the darkening sky loomed above. Each ray of light outlined his features, from the messy hair to the sharp lines of his collarbone. I wanted nothing more than to sleep, but he seemed determined to rage on until he won.

"You know what you need, Lilah?" His voice had darkened so that a quiver passed along my spine, "You need humility. Really, it's an easy thing to grasp once you've practiced. You need to accept that there's such a thing as respect and that you aren't the greatest person out there."

My eyes bulged; I was unable to comprehend his blindness to his own hypocrisy. Trying to make him aware of it, though, would only cause him to take a defensive stance. Instead of allowing the anger to control me, I wanted to try to help him. I wanted peace; fighting was a waste of time.

"I was wrong to argue with you, Revelin. You're right, and so clever," I said, a small smile so genuine erupting upon my face that even my own mother wouldn't be able to detect the falsity. "Let's forget this."

His eyes squinted in disbelief for a moment, but he swiftly elevated his chin and set his shoulders back, feeling accomplished. "Ha, I knew you would cave eventually."

I nodded and we descended into the room below the fountain. According to Revelin, before anything further could happen, we would need to map out a plan. I was glad he knew the structure of the inside of the palace, or else there was no way we would be able to sneak in and rescue my family.

Keeping the entrance open so that some light could flood into the room, we each sat uncomfortably on the edge of the moss bed. I could hardly see his face, but I knew his mind was reeling.

"Wait..." he began, turning his head to face me, "That

apology wasn't real. You're trying to trick me."

I grinned. But once again my mind wandered to Andrew, Ali, and Nico. "Listen, Revelin. We need to make a plan to save my family, and we have to do it quickly. Tonight, if we can. We'll be too visible during the day."

After a minute of being unable to tear his eyes away from me, scrutinizing my every movement, he finally sighed. He stood and paced the room again, thinking deeply. Every so often he glanced in my direction, obviously trying to solve a conflict.

"Here's the thing," he said, "I don't think we should save your family. Remember how Tara told you that Ali said the Gift is the most important? Well, I agree with her. It isn't worth the risk to sneak right into Casimir's grasp just to release your family and friends. We need to escape over the wall. There are times when you have to make sacrifices for others, Lilah. But the hardest thing to accept is that there are also times when you have to let others sacrifice themselves…for you."

Even though it was a conceited viewpoint, Revelin's words bored into me, instantly making me want to believe him, but then I remembered he was half Deceiver.

"You don't understand. The Gift is part of me, right? So instead of letting other people suffer, the best thing to do would be to sacrifice myself. If I'm gone, the Gift is gone. I don't have a child that it would pass down to, so it would just disappear forever. Casimir would have nothing to search for, so he would free the townspeople," I said, this new idea seeming like the best out of anything we'd come up with so far. It's not that I wanted to die; it's just that I was willing to face death for people that I loved, and really, wouldn't it be just another great adventure?

"That's not fair though!" He nearly shouted, turning sharply and grabbing my arms so that I was forced to stand and look at him.

"What are you talking about? Why isn't it fair?" I replied, yanking my arms away.

"It's not fair for the... the people you leave behind. It would be so selfish. There's another way," he said, leaving me to pace again, "there's a passage that leads into the prison that Casimir doesn't know about, but it's small. I don't know if anyone will be able to fit through it."

Instantly, my eyes lit up and I dashed to the staircase, "It's worth a try, now c'mon. We don't have any time to lose."

8 Welcome Home, Revelin

Revelin glanced at the patch of moss on the floor, clearly longing to sleep, but shook his head, giving up, as he turned to follow me. Though we were both exhausted, I was determined to find that hidden passage and try to save as many people as we could. Perhaps it would have been wiser to wait another day or week, but my impulsive nature was urging me to leave *now*.

We waited until the sun disappeared, then I climbed the staircase with Revelin on my heels and dug my fingers into the grass to stand up. Once we neared the bushes, his eyes widened as he pointed at my necklace. I glanced down to find it strangely glowing again, and my reaction was to be just as surprised as he.

"That's the…" he said. But I didn't find out what he was going to say, because before he could finish the sentence, I clamped my hand over his mouth. We had to keep as silent as possible; Deceivers were bound to be around every corner.

I shook my head, motioning for him to stay quiet. He arrogantly removed my hand but decided not to speak. After parting the bushes and peeking through, I whispered that the street was clear and we skulked into the town.

Strings of moonlight looped along the stone streets and houses, lighting the area enough to see, but still leaving enough shadows to cause me to shudder. A silent yearning clung to the air like the breath of a forgotten soul, begging to return to life, but trapped in the inescapable clutch of death. Revelin somehow managed to keep a perfect distance behind me: just close enough that I couldn't tell him to catch up and just far enough that I couldn't tell him to back away.

My ears were straining for the slightest of sounds, but Deceivers were difficult to hear—especially at night, when they prowled around searching for any curfew-breakers. As we reached the end of a house halfway to the palace, though, my heart leaped into my throat.

Before I could react, Revelin whisked forward, wrapping an arm around my waist and covering my mouth with his hand. He soundlessly pulled me against his body and pressed against the wall of the house where shadows hid us from view. The only thing that made us visible was the faint light coming from my necklace.

Seconds later, a tall, thin Deceiver with gangly arms and straight silver hair turned the corner and crept along the street in front of us. A metal nightstick was planted firmly in his right hand. He was just a few yards away, facing downward and listening intently. His pace was slow and it continued to get slower with each step.

Revelin and I dared not speak, dared not move, dared not breathe. The Deceiver's steps became agonizingly slow until he came to a complete halt in front of us. He was still facing the street, but suddenly his head whipped to the side.

A pair of glowing, icy white eyes clawed into me, causing my skin to grow cold, raking at my conscious mind. Revelin instinctively dug his fingers into my waist, my hands trembling slightly as the Deceiver stood motionless.

The Deceiver's foot moved one step in our direction, the moonlight glinting on the metal nightstick. He turned to face us completely, and it seemed as though he would lunge forward any moment.

My lungs burned from the lack of oxygen as I forced myself not to breathe, but the Deceiver looked as though he had no intention of walking away. Finally when I felt my lungs about to burst for air, the Deceiver shrugged and disappeared down a dark alley.

Revelin instantly removed his hand and I took heavy breaths, trying to keep them as quiet as I could. He released his grip around my waist and the color flushed back into his face as the oxygen reentered his lungs. We exchanged a look, realizing we were lucky to be alive, and continued to the palace.

We were more careful this time: Revelin stayed right beside me and we had to hide frequently as Deceivers madly searched for us. After what seemed like hours, we arrived at the lilac tree that marked the boundary between Casimir's kingdom and the town.

The winding branches twisted elegantly, reaching toward the sky.

The silver floor beamed gloriously in the moonlight, turning a pearly white. Casimir's palace, however, was still ugly with its many shadows cringing away from the light. Revelin and I stood against the trunk of the tree, observing the grounds in front of us. I gazed at the dozens of Deceivers that guarded the palace doors,

"There are too many Deceivers," I whispered almost inaudibly, "how're we supposed to get around them? The area's too open: they'll definitely see us."

I turned my head to find Revelin smirking wildly, obviously thinking himself to be very clever. He motioned for me to follow him as he bent down beside the trunk of the tree. After a minute or so of looking around to make sure nobody was watching, he began lifting up a flat stone about three feet wide. The stone pulled away to reveal a small hole in the ground just big enough for Revelin to fit through, which seemed to drop down for a few feet, then turn sharply towards the palace.

It reminded me of the room below the fountain, and I wondered if my great-grandfather dug this tunnel, too. But how did Revelin know about it?

"Well, this is it: the passage to the prison," he whispered, reluctantly lowering himself into the hole. Once reaching the bottom, he ducked to crawl headfirst through the tunnel.

I took a final breath of fresh air and followed him into the darkness, dragging the stone back to cover the opening. I ducked and crawled after him, my knees and arms sinking into the damp earth. Roots scraped my elbows, the thick mud sloshed between my fingers, and dozens of beetles scattered each time I moved forward. Thankfully there were no spiders; I didn't mind the beetles…but Revelin flinched each time one touched him.

There was no way that somebody large could fit through this; and my stomach knotted when I realized that Mr. Aljoy would not be able to come back with us…and maybe not even my own parents.

After suddenly noticing that I could see Revelin's legs quite a few feet ahead of me, I looked down to find my necklace radiating milky white light. So I hadn't been imagining it; the webbed strings really did glow. But why?

"Revelin," I said, feeling safe enough to talk because we were below the ground.

"Yeah?" He replied, still crawling quickly along the tunnel.

"What were you going to say earlier, about my necklace? And how did you find this tunnel?" I asked.

"Now's not the time, Lilah. I'll tell you later," he answered, slowing his pace a little. "I think we're almost there. Listen to me, this is the plan:

"The tunnel opens into the floor of the prison cell. Deceivers are everywhere outside the cell, even some that aren't blind. We'll have to do this silently and quickly. If we make one mistake—do anything wrong—you'll be in Casimir's hands in minutes." He stopped suddenly, moving to crouch below the opening into the cell and facing me.

"I'm going to open this," he said, lowering his voice to a whisper, "and look into the cell. I'll motion over your family and friends one by one, and you'll lead them back down the tunnel. Don't stop for anything, okay Lilah? I know you'll want to help if someone gets left behind, but that's not an option."

His legs extended until he was crouching and his hands grasped the stone that would open into the floor of the prison.

"Revelin, wait," I began, not sure what I'd planned on saying.

He glanced down at me with a powerfully impatient scowl.

A lump formed in my throat, almost stopping me from speaking. "I trust you," I whispered. I did? My words shocked me just as much as they shocked Revelin.

He hesitated for a second, but then a genuine grin escaped and illuminated his entire face. I didn't smile, but my cheeks flushed slightly as I nodded for him to continue; we needed to finish this as soon as possible.

Inches at a time, he lifted and slid the thick stone over to the side, revealing a dimly lit room. I could see nothing but a candle twitching weakly in a lantern that hung against the wall. The hole seemed to be on the far edge of the prison cell, because as Revelin hesitantly peeked into the room, he faced away from the wall. Immediately, he ducked again to speak to me.

"Everyone's in there: Mr. and Mrs. Aljoy, your family, Nico, Ali and her brothers and sister," he said so quietly that I could hardly hear. "Most of them are asleep, but I can get that boy to wake them up."

Once again his head rose and after a few seconds, he waved his hand a little. I heard the quiet sound of scampering feet as Revelin pressed himself against the wall of the tunnel. He raised his arms and soundlessly lowered down Ali's red-haired brother Henry.

Henry's face was pale with fear as I placed a finger on my lips, showing him not to speak. I clutched him into a hug and his muscles relaxed. Gently grasping his chubby hand, I moved him behind me in the tunnel, waiting for Revelin to lower the next person.

Henry must have woken everyone, because Ali's two other siblings, Alf and Tina, quietly scuttled in after him, their eyes wide and their lips tight. I pulled them both into a reassuring hug and Revelin motioned for me to start crawling back through the tunnel. Henry tugged on my hand, trying to pull me back, but something kept me still. Unable to understand why I couldn't leave, I waited and listened. There was something that was missing, something that was tying me to the spot with an invisible bond.

Revelin grabbed the next child from the prison and placed him in front of me. Instantly, the thing holding me back dissolved as I embraced Andrew, my fingers locked in his messy black hair. His round cheeks danced in the light of my necklace as he wrapped spindly arms around my waist.

"You came for us," he whispered.

"Of course I did; I always will," I replied, squeezing his hand as I began leading them through the tunnel back toward the lilac tree.

As the four children followed me, I glanced back just in time to see both Ali and Nico land in the tunnel before they were too far away and faded into the darkness. A sigh of relief washed through me.

"Look, the necklace glows," Henry pointed, eyes wide with wonder. Alf and Tina exchanged an innocent giggle and Andrew mirrored Henry's surprise. A small smile flickered on my lips; I admired how quickly they could release all troubles and how they thought the simplest things were magical.

The muffled sounds of hands and knees swiping across the dirt multiplied as I guessed Revelin started to lead the others down the tunnel. Did he get everyone? Mr. and Mrs. Aljoy, and my parents? I refused to think that they might not be able to fit.

The dim light from my necklace bent upward as we reached the end of the tunnel, and I turned to find four smiling faces staring at me, waiting to be free.

That was it, then. We'd escaped.

I stood and slid the stone to reveal the starry sky above and the welcoming, purple-blossomed boughs of the lilac tree. One by one, I lifted the others out of the hole. As I was about to follow them out, Revelin appeared through the darkness. His radiant eyes hid too many secrets for me to find the single one I was looking for: who was left in the prison?

"Keep going, Lilah. C'mon, don't look back," he ordered, turning me towards the hole so that I couldn't see who was behind him.

"You left them, didn't you?" I whispered, still facing away from him. My back was rigid, knowing there were people missing.

"It's okay, we're here," Ali's sweet voice echoed from further down the tunnel. I obeyed and climbed out of the hole, knowing that the Deceivers would notice the missing prisoners and be on our trail in minutes.

As I stood and leaned against the tree, I immediately became aware of the eerie silence that clouded the air: Andrew and the others were nowhere to be seen. As I used the shadows of the tree to conceal myself, my eyes darted to the side.

Two Deceivers sprang from behind a house and grasped onto my wrists with such speed that I was nearly knocked off my feet. I opened my mouth to yell, which would warn Revelin to stay in the tunnel, but a cold hand dug into my face restraining me from speaking. He, Ali, and Nico appeared from the hole in the ground and were instantly grabbed by a few other Deceivers. So Mr. and Mrs. Aljoy...my parents...they were all still in the prison. Frustrated, I tried to struggle out of the Deceivers' grip.

Revelin kicked and punched, but the burly Deceivers didn't even flinch. Nico struggled and tried to slip away, even though we all knew it was useless. Ali broke into silent tears which rolled down her cheeks and soaked her lips.

No, this couldn't be happening! Not now, not when we were so close to freedom. How did they find us? They must have heard us.

Andrew and the other children were all held off to the side, and I recognized Timoria as the Deceiver angrily holding Ali, her thin lips pulled into a smirk. Her rat-like face looked twisted and devious in the moonlight.

"Let the children go," she sneered. "We only need these four."

The Deceivers hesitantly released the children, who fearfully disappeared into the town, except for Andrew. He stood courageously in front of Timoria, his little chin raised to look her in the eyes.

The Deceiver that was previously holding the children stomped threateningly in front of Andrew. In fear, he jumped and looked at me, wondering if he could help.

I jerked my head to the side, telling him to go with the other children; he was so much like me sometimes that it was hard to believe. Reluctantly, he took a few steps back before turning and disappearing into the darkness of the town.

I exchanged looks with Revelin, Nico, and Ali; silently apologizing for dragging them all into this. The eight Deceivers, two holding each of us, all patiently waited for Timoria's orders.

"Ah yes, Lilah, I knew you would show up eventually. It's hard to ignore a death threat to your family. And now I'll be the one to hand the Gift over to Casimir," she grinned, causing my eyebrows to furrow in anger. Sometimes I forgot that she was blind, her hearing was so advanced that she knew of everything happening around her.

"And who do we have here?" she laughed, turning to Revelin.

"If it isn't the traitor himself. Finally decided to come home to your father? Or…were you protecting the one you love?"

Revelin's face turned from furious to shocked, his eyes wide as he freed his mouth for a few seconds: "I would never come back to my father. And I don't *love* her. I don't *love* anyone." The sudden pallor of his face at the last words, however, suggested a lie.

Whom was Timoria talking about? Whom did Revelin supposedly love?

"Don't think I didn't know it was you who knocked me unconscious with a nightstick a while ago when I was chasing her. You saved her, and are still trying to. And it's not because of the Gift. If it were, you wouldn't care and would've already turned her in to Casimir. It's because *she's* the person who *has* the Gift," Timoria said. Her expression was caught between remorseful fear and an evil smirk.

I gazed wide-eyed at Revelin as I realized it was *me* who Timoria was accusing him of loving. At first, a laugh almost formed in my throat because I knew how ridiculous that was; if Revelin had any sort of feeling toward me, it was hatred. He shook his head and looked away, refusing to make eye contact with me.

Could Timoria be telling the truth? It seemed almost funny, yes, and I hoped it was a lie. But when I thought about it, why *was* Revelin helping me? With a sigh, I easily dismissed it all.

Timoria's rat-face seemed to be convulsing in confusion: she turned nervously back to the palace and then toward the town.

Finally, her fear got the best of her and she motioned for the others to follow her. While we returned to the palace, the Deceivers and Timoria leading me and Ali in the front, I managed to wrench my mouth free from restraint.

"Look at me Timoria!" I said, causing her to jump with surprise and turn to me.

The group stopped behind Timoria, all shocked that I'd spoken. The Deceiver whose hand was previously on my mouth tried to silence me by covering it again.

"Release her mouth, Damon," Timoria crooned in her sickeningly kind voice. The ugly, swollen-faced Deceiver, Damon, grunted and returned his hand to my wrist.

"Let the others go; you have no reason to keep them. I'm the one with the Gift," I said steadily.

Timoria gave Ali to the other large Deceiver who was holding her, and slinked over to me. The way she crept around just made her seem more rat-like. Her short, thin figure could be mistaken for that of a child if you couldn't see her face. She stopped just inches in front of me, tilting her head to the side to give me a curious stare. Shadows bordered the expressionless holes that were her eyes, casting fear into the observer even though she was blind.

Ali whipped her head backwards, momentarily breaking her mouth free before being silenced again, "No! We're staying with you, Lilah. Through it all."

Her words sank into me: Casimir would start using me once we reached the palace. It could be the beginning...the beginning of destruction. But why did I feel that Casimir was afraid, being forced to do something he didn't want to do?

"Oh, how sweet. Trying to be gallant, are you?" she said to Ali and me, frowning almost fearfully. "Your kindness won't help you here. The only way to survive is to save *yourself.* Don't you understand? Stop trying to *help* each other, stop trying to be *brave.*"

She turned and faced the palace, breathing heavily, that look of fear flashing across her face again. Why did she seem so scared all the time?

"No, I have to take the four of you back. Specific orders from Casimir," she said, stumbling a little as she returned to Ali, the look of fear completely vanished.

Her words settled nauseatingly in the pit of my stomach, and I felt like crying, but of course I suppressed the tears. I couldn't show the others that I was considering defeat; it would strip them of whatever hope they still clung to. Nico nodded reassuringly at me as I glanced back at him, and Revelin stared fixedly at me, his words from earlier ringing through my mind again:

The hardest thing to accept is that there are also times when you have to let others sacrifice themselves...for you.

At first I thought that was a conceited viewpoint, but suddenly I understood the true meaning. Watching Ali, Nico, and Revelin suffer for me was definitely more difficult than sacrificing myself.

Ali glanced back at me, her tears gliding down over the Deceiver's hand that was covering her mouth. The Deceiver could have snapped her thin body like a twig, and our vulnerability against these huge men only angered me more. Nico and Revelin tried to appear brave, but I knew they feared what would happen in Casimir's grasp just as much as I did.

As we arrived at the tall palace doors, Timoria turned to smirk at us before hurriedly knocking on the smooth metal. Slowly, the doors creaked open and revealed an unpleasant atmosphere.

"Welcome home," Timoria whispered mockingly in Revelin's ear, giggling as the Deceivers led us into the palace and closed the doors behind us.

9 The Gift

After my eyes adjusted to the darkness, I could make out a long foyer with a silver staircase at the end climbing steeply upward. A ghostly chandelier dangled from the ceiling, radiating a dim blue light similar to that of the lamppost outside. My toes dug into a thin gray rug that—instead of feeling comforting—seemed to drain the hope out of me and absorb it.

Dozens of Deceivers stood along the walls of the foyer, protecting dozens of closed doors that led into unknown areas. Keeping perfectly still as they listened to every sound, they could have been mistaken for statues.

Since there were no windows, it was impossible for outside light and fresh air to leak in : my lungs seemed to contract. The Deceivers, hidden from light, wore no hoods and many silver-haired heads turned as Timoria made her presence known.

"Look, everyone, at what I've dragged in," she boasted like a child, twirling dramatically in a circle to point at us: "Revelin, the traitor himself, and…no other than Lilah Keeper, *the Gift*."

Gasps and sneering cheers erupted from the Deceivers as they left their guarding of the doors and crowded around us. Everyone praised Timoria, laughing as they heard a description of me from a non-blind Deceiver.

"She's incredibly *small*, and *thin*, and *weak-looking*. And those *enormous* bug eyes…and those *dirt-covered* cheeks…oh sorry, those are freckles," the non-blind Deceiver chuckled, receiving a hoot of laughter from the others. I closed my eyes so as to block out the scene as Nico tried to lunge at them, but was of course restrained, which only caused more evil snickering.

While Nico, Ali, Revelin, and I were still controlled by the Deceivers, Timoria pushed coldly through the crowd and they dispersed back to their guard duties. She seemed intent on finding Casimir.

My breath grew shallower with each step we took toward the great silver staircase, dreading what could be waiting at the top. I tried to catch Revelin's eye as he glared ahead, still struggling against the Deceivers' grip. Wasn't there some way we could get out of this? It didn't seem possible; it couldn't be happening…this was what my father feared the most, and he was still locked in that prison, unaware, unable to help me.

But, Casimir couldn't *make* me dream. I could just say that the Gift had worn out or didn't work anymore. As these ideas filtered through me, the Deceivers pushed us up the stairs, toward a great black door at the top. Timoria stretched out her arm to knock: each sound of her fist pounding the door sending painful throbs through my body.

Ali had stopped crying, and her eyes were wide with shock. Nico was breathing deeply with anticipation, and Revelin's eyebrows were tightly furrowed as if he would burst open at any second and yell. I remained rigid, unable to outwardly express the numerous conflicting emotions bubbling within me. We all knew who waited behind that door.

Timoria giggled as the black door crawled open just enough to reveal the face of a woman. Her long, silky black hair, dark eyes, and beautiful face caused me to jump: she looked so similar to Revelin. It was Lucetta.

"What—what do you want?" she stuttered quietly, her eyes bulging as she noticed Revelin. He returned the look of surprise, the tightness of his eyebrows receding as he stared at his mother. She then glanced at me and an unexpected softness passed over her face…a look of pity.

"Lucy," Timoria croaked guiltily, obviously remembering their friendship and how it ended, "I need to speak with Casimir. I've brought him…the Gift."

With an emotionless face except for her suddenly watery eyes, Lucetta pulled the door open and stepped away.

"Well, what are you waiting for?" Timoria hissed impatiently, "Push them into the room, and leave…except for Damon and Marcus: come with us."

"But Timoria," muttered one of the Deceivers, "we captured them too, we deserve some recognition from Cas—"

"I DON'T CARE! *OUT!*" she shrieked, her bushy hair standing wildly on end. The Deceivers jumped, untied all our bonds, released us, and scrambled back down the staircase. I rubbed my wrists: the skin was red from being held tightly. I could clearly see the faces of Ali, Nico, and Revelin all turned toward me, but I was focused on the room, trying to see Casimir. I couldn't face my friends after all the things I dragged them through.

The four of us were shoved into the room, followed by the swollen-faced Damon and a burly Deceiver with short, silver hair who I guessed was Marcus. Timoria was fuming in front of us, cringing as she passed Lucetta and slamming the black door closed behind us.

Instantly, a gush of cold air slapped my face, and it took a minute for my eyes to adjust to the extreme darkness. A single light shuddered in the corner, casting bluish beams onto a slick silver floor. Instead of being smooth, however, the silver was shaped like triangular tiles.

Ali, Nico, and I instinctively huddled together while Revelin stood off to the side, inaudibly muttering to his mother. The tone of his voice was laced with anger, and it seemed to be the only sound in the room.

The four walls were black as charcoal, as if we were surrounded by an endless pit. A few stiff couches lined the walls, and an elegant wooden table held a vase of wilted lilac flowers from the tree outside that marked the boundary.

Timoria had wandered to the darkest part of the room, and she was grinning when she returned to Damon's side. Out of the shadows emerged the man we all anticipated: towering, lean and ghostly against the black background. I nearly jumped when he stepped into the light: he wasn't the same.

Two hollow dents replaced his cheeks, sunken eyes were nearly swollen shut, and his bones protruded prominently. Each rickety step shuddered through his body, his face wincing and twisting, his fingers trembling. He stumbled over to the table and latched onto it for support, his breathing labored and quick. The silver lines of his eyebrows quivered painfully as he grasped his chest. He could very well have been mistaken for an old man of eighty, instead of forty.

"Timoria…quick, see if she has it," he croaked, pointing in my direction.

"Dad…?" Revelin said in disbelief and dislike, staring at the skeleton that was his father.

Casimir ignored his son's plea for recognition, his face cruel and determined, even though he was frail and weak. Timoria approached me and I stepped back, only to be restrained by Damon again before I could speak in protest.

She pawed blindly around my neck, grinning when her fingers closed on the chain of my necklace. She carefully removed it, as if it were made of the most fragile glass and she feared it would break. I was confused…why did he want the necklace?

Revelin lashed out again, diving for Timoria, but was pinned to the floor by Marcus before he could reach her. Nico and Ali, sharing my confusion, huddled together beside me.

"No, Timoria! You don't understand what you're doing. Think…think about the consequences. Think about the people it will affect," Revelin said, squirming on the ground.

"But my daughter…she must be protected," Timoria whispered to herself, moving without hesitation to hand the necklace to Casimir. Timoria had a daughter?

Greedily, he grasped the necklace and lowered it onto his neck, sinking to a crouch from the weight as I had experienced when first wearing it. When he stood to recover, he laughed darkly as a sickly change began to twist his features.

His body seemed to become younger: His cheeks filled out and his eyelids returned to normal; his flesh became healthier and brighter, and his wrinkles flattened to reveal the face of a handsome man. His previously stringy, whitish hair that was plastered to his head with grease shortened and darkened to a deep gray. It was as if half of the years of his life disappeared, and he was forty again.

Ali and Nico jumped back, and Revelin shouted words I couldn't hear. My head throbbed with such intensity that I slackened into Damon's grip, reality crumbling away like sand between my fingers. It was as if pieces of my brain were being plucked away.

My muscles wouldn't move; I could only watch as Casimir advanced with such speed toward me that it was like an illusion.

He cackled which caused Lucetta, who was already cowering in the corner, to stifle a cry. Casimir stood before me, his blind eyes twinkling with youth, his full lips curved into a grin.

"Do you feel that, Lilah? That pain in your head? Yes, that special little head of yours, capable of creating anything with a simple dream. Capable of creating whatever you desire.

"You see, Lilah, back when your great-grandfather dreamed us to become these Deceivers, these *monsters*, he dreamed the worst punishment for my grandfather, the one who truly wanted to steal the Gift.

"He dreamed that my grandfather and all his future descendants would be cursed with this—this flaw: this flaw of decay, of becoming older quicker than we're supposed to. Of shortened time…of shortened life. It started when I turned twenty, and I appeared to be thirty. Then just a moment ago, look at what I was. An old man. Look at what your *kind* has done to me. To my father. To my…*son*," he said, spitting out the last word as if it were riddled with disease. So Revelin, being Casimir's son, also had the curse? Then he, too, would be aging more quickly than he should in a few years.

Revelin tried to stand again and confront his father, but Marcus was unyielding.

"But," he continued, "thanks to this necklace, created some time ago by your great-grandfather, there is a way…a way that I can return the life that was stolen from me. This necklace…this blessed necklace…has the ability to eliminate whatever the wearer believes is corrupt in themselves. The words carved into the metal circle reveal that, if you're bright enough to figure it out.

"Whenever somebody with the Gift wears it, a part of their bad dreams melts into it, for safe keeping. Your great-grandfather called it the Dream-Catcher, and used it to keep away the bad dreams, by locking them in the necklace as if it were a vault. But little did he know that the Dream-Catcher works for others as well. When I wear it, my curse disappears. However, Lilah, your father hid the necklace from me in an attempt to destroy me, and I suppose he decided to give it to you. Thankfully though, I found it just in time." He paced in front of me with the high energy of a boy.

"You feel that pain because those bad dreams that you stored in the Dream-Catcher are a *part of you*. And when my curse leaves me, entering into it, they're mixed with that part of you. But your pain doesn't mean anything to me. See how I thrive? *That* is what matters the most."

He laughed again, the horrid sound causing the throbbing in my head to intensify. I glanced at Nico and Ali, who were pressed against a wall as Timoria threatened to hit them with a nightstick if they moved. Nico's mouth hung open and his eyebrows furrowed in pity, and Ali's silent tears dripped off her small chin as she tried to restrain herself from helping me.

"Lilah's great-grandfather didn't create the flaw on purpose; it was an accident! They can't control their dreams, Casimir, they form like thoughts, unable to be changed—" Nico explained, his face contorting as he watched me slump to the floor when Damon realized I was no longer a threat. At the moment I could only move my eyes, the splitting pain in my head restraining me from further motion.

"Ah, is that what you told him, Lilah? That you can't control your dreams?" Casimir said. "She lied to you, boy. You see, she can control them, but she probably hasn't found out how yet. Her father didn't know how, either. But *I* do. Now, Timoria, if you would be so kind as to silence the children."

With swift movements, Timoria withdrew two strips of cloth from her pockets and tied them around the mouths of Nico and Ali as Damon held them in place.

"You're going to regret this," Nico managed to say before the cloth was tied tightly.

"I can assure you, little *boy*, that I will *not*," Casimir chuckled.

He ordered Timoria and Damon to grab Nico and Ali, and drag them to the center of the room. I watched helplessly from the floor as my friends were tied together with rope and the two Deceivers drew objects from their pockets that caused my already exhausted body to shrivel. Needle-like silver daggers sprouted from the hands of the Deceivers as they circled Nico and Ali.

"As you can see, your friends are in a *dangerous* situation. Now, it would only be natural for *you*…who are exceptionally *gallant*…" Casimir said with his upper lip raised in a snarl, "to want to save them, right? So, cooperate, and I promise you they will be released, unharmed."

"I'm no hero, Casimir," I managed to say. However, nobody seemed to have heard.

I then understood why Timoria had said it was Casimir's specific orders that the four of us were to be brought back to the kingdom. He wanted to control me by threatening to harm Nico and Ali.

"You're a *coward*!" Revelin shouted from somewhere underneath Marcus, which only caused him to be pinned down even more harshly.

Casimir ignored his son, watching as I struggled to sit up and lean against the wall. The pain had somewhat subsided, but my legs still refused to support me. What could Casimir possibly want? But I knew…I knew. He wanted my dreams, of course.

He crouched just inches in front of me, his blind eyes boring into my face, tilting his head to the side mockingly, "And what do you think you were doing, trying to steal my prisoners? That's not wise, child. And now, you will dream for me. Or else, your friends will suffer."

Revelin tried to shout at his father again, but Marcus tied a cloth over his mouth and bound his feet and wrists together. I caught a glimpse of his radiant blue eyes before Marcus dragged him to the center with the others. A flashback of seeing him on the carriage all those years ago crossed my mind and my stomach twisted. Casimir didn't show the slightest bit of care that his son was being treated as just another enemy.

Ali's and Nico's eyes were glued to me, silently begging me

not to obey Casimir, while Revelin stared loathingly at his father. Although my body was in an immobile state, my mind was still capable of forming a plan.

"You're afraid," I said simply.

Casimir stood to look down on me, raised an eyebrow, and then threw his head back in laughter, "*Stupid* girl! What are you talking about? I'm not afraid of you."

"Not of *me*, no, but you *are* afraid of something. I can see it in your eyes. Ever since you first showed yourself to the townspeople, I've always seen it. I know somebody's forcing you to do this. Somebody's putting you up to this, somebody else who wants the Gift. Whoever is doing it, Casimir, you don't have to listen to them. There's always another way." I knew that every word I was saying was a lie, but I had to distract him for as long as possible.

"Nobody's forcing me to do anything; *I* want this," he said. "I want the power of the Gift, just as my father before me. You're a fool, Lilah, for not seeing it. *You* have the power to do, change, or create anything you want to. But now it's *mine*. Now that I finally have you, *I* can do, change, or create anything I want to."

"But look at your son; don't you see how he rebels against you? He rebels because he can see beneath your surface. He can see that you, too, wish to rebel and don't want this power. And why would you sacrifice your own son in order to obtain power for yourself? Don't you feel any shame?" I asked, unable to think of anything else to distract him.

If I could just grab the necklace from him, the curse would return and he would turn into a powerless old man again…. But then what? Damon and Timoria still possessed the daggers, and Marcus still guarded the door.

"Shame is weakness," he hissed. He seemed to know I was attempting to distract him.

"There's another way—"

"*Enough*!" He screeched nervously, grabbing my arms and yanking me to a standing position. "Enough of these distractions. Now, since you're too stupid to figure it out, I have to show you how to control the dreams."

The muscles in my legs, however, were still unresponsive and I leaned on the couch beside me in order to remain upright. Though he continually insulted me, I couldn't peel my eyes from the prisoners tied together in the center of the room. There must be a way out…but the windowless room showed no escape other than the guarded door, and even then there was no way I could rescue Nico, Ali, and Revelin. I wouldn't leave without them…I couldn't.

Casimir wandered toward me, pacing around me in a circle, staring intently at my head, "To begin, do you know how the Gift came about, Lilah? Do you know how that special dreamy talent of yours came into existence?"

"It was given to a man long ago to help him during a great war," I replied, recalling the story my father told me.

He chuckled, shaking his head, "*Given* to a man who needed help? During a war? So, maybe I could just whine until somebody gives me the Gift. No, it wasn't that simple. Did it ever cross your mind *where* this man got the Gift?"

The question had, actually, been bothering me since the day my father passed the Gift down to me, but I felt that he didn't have the answer, so nobody would. But how did Casimir know this much?

"You're fifteen, yes? Did you ever wonder why you were so advanced, so much more intelligent than the other children your age? Your range of understanding is comparable with an adult's, yet you never took the time to realize it, which shows you're still just a child.

"The Gift isn't named that because it was *given* to a man; it's called that because it's a special talent that only a few people had. Yes, it began long ago, but not with one man. It was a certain group of people, there were quite a few of them, and they had advanced brain abilities. Advanced ESP—extra-sensory perception. They were all humble and selfless, and they refrained from using the Gift because they worried it would cause destruction.

"You see, when an average person is sleeping, their conscious brain shuts off, and their unconscious, fantasy-driven brain takes control. But your logical mind *doesn't* shut off, and your ESP literally manipulates people and your surroundings to accommodate the events of your dreams.

"All the other people without this brainpower were, naturally, jealous of the people with the Gift. So they foolishly killed them off in an attempt to take the Gift for themselves. But one escaped the grasp of the fools and melted into their lifestyle, hiding the Gift from them. That one is your ancestor, Lilah. The Gift then gradually passed down generations, but it never multiplied past one family.

"Your father never *passed down* the Gift; you've always had it. It just didn't work until you were about ten years old, when you became capable of reasoning and mature thoughts. Not every child receives it; only the firstborn does, and that's the reason why your brother doesn't have it. The Gift deteriorates when you reach about forty, and that's why your father no longer possesses it." Casimir finished, observing me as I absorbed his information, as I lost my balance again and toppled to the floor.

This whole race of gifted, selfless people, and I was the only one remaining? It must not have fully developed yet, because from what I could tell, I was not the most humble person. If anybody, Ali should have the Gift: she was the only person I knew capable of such selflessness. And of the history of the Gift, why did Casimir know and not my father? Did my father just keep it a secret?

I sat, speechless, on the cold floor, thousands of questions swimming in my mind like crazed fish. Casimir snickered at me, slinking around me as he watched my brain grinding.

Nico mirrored my expression of shock and Ali's head was shaking in disbelief, all struggling to comprehend the story we never knew. Revelin, probably having heard the story many times from his father, remained angry as he tried without success to break his bonds. An uncomfortable silence settled, as if Casimir's circular pacing would eventually close in on me, suffocating me.

His deep voice bellowed through the windowless room, ringing through my ears and causing Lucetta to cower even further into the shadows.

"And now, Lilah, you *will* dream."

10 The Deceiver's Heir

Shadows from the bodies around me fanned out, phantom-like, on the silver floor; and I gazed as the outlines of my ancestors being killed seemed to take shape in them. A few hours had passed since we were first captured, and Nico, Ali, and Revelin sat slumped together on the floor, their backs resting against each other's. Revelin and I hadn't slept much in the past days, and it must have been early morning already, but both of us fought to stay awake.

"You need to have confidence; don't fear anything. You *brat*, it's so *simple!*" Casimir shrieked for the hundredth time, staring at me from down his long, bony nose.

"If you gave me the Dream-Catcher and bad dreams couldn't occur, then I wouldn't *have* anything to fear—" I mumbled from my slouched position on the floor, my back leaning on the side of a couch for support.

Timoria and Damon still circled my friends with daggers in hand, though more sleepily. Marcus stood, immobile, in front of

135

the door; a nightstick at the ready. Nico couldn't remove his eyes from me, while Ali struggled to keep hers open, her finger nervously tracing the triangle shapes on the floor.

"NO! I need it. Now, this is your final chance. We'll start with something easy: Dream that I have my eyesight. Or else Timoria will, let's say… play with the pretty little face of your friend Ali," Casimir snarled, his crooked teeth clicking. He whirled to face Timoria, his silver cloak flapping against his boot-clad ankles.

With crazed features and a high-pitched cackle, Timoria traced the tip of her dagger along Ali's cheekbone, slicing a cut in her skin. After a muffled whimper, Ali somehow remained calm, although she tried to bury herself in the crevice between Revelin and Nico. Defensively, Nico tried to throw himself in front of the dagger so as to help Ali, but the bonds held him in place.

"*Stop!*" I screeched, dragging my body to a kneeling position, my head still reeling with dizziness. "I'll…I'll do it."

Then, a brilliant plan formed in my mind: If I tried hard enough, I could just dream that we escaped, and were all safely in the room beneath the fountain. Casimir would never guess that I was capable of such elaborate dreams…he thought I could only imagine simple things.

"Ah," Casimir smirked, "good girl."

With another flick of his blasted silver cloak, he turned to pace as I crawled and relaxed onto the stiff couch, preparing myself for sleep. I could picture it easily: The damp moss bed, the four of us standing securely in the underground room, not a Deceiver in sight.

"Listen carefully, Lilah," Casimir said, his voice a dark mumble, "my Deceivers are quick, and do not make mistakes. If you dream of anything besides my eyesight, your friends will be dead before you even wake up."

As reinforcement, Damon chuckled as he grabbed a handful of Nico's hair, wrenching his head back and placing the dagger just centimeters from his neck.

"I said *stop*!" I shouted, nearly falling from the couch.

"Do what I say, and everyone will be unharmed. You have my word," said Casimir, forcing my shoulders back with his cold hands so that I was glued to the couch. "I'll wake you in half-an-hour, and should I not have my eyesight, we'll keep trying until you get it."

"If you do so much as touch them again, your eyesight won't be an issue. Your *life* will be the real thing to worry about," I whispered into Casimir's face which was inches from my own.

"*Shut up*. If you want Nico to live, I would suggest you stop talking and start dreaming. *Now*," Casimir ordered. He backed away and watched me from above, waiting.

Unable to form a plan, think of an escape route, or say anything else to distract Casimir, I squeezed my eyes shut, willing myself to dream. If I didn't return his eyesight, he would kill my friends. After all, giving back his eyesight wasn't that disastrous. I could only hope that my dream became reality immediately, instead of a week later as it did last time.

I focused directly on Casimir's face: Bright, aware, acute eyes that were rid of blindness, darting around and easily seeing the objects before him. Within a few minutes, the room—silent as death—lulled me into a light sleep.

My dream went as planned and Casimir's face was grinning wickedly in front of me, his eyes alive and vigilant. He scanned the room, absorbing the scene around him as if he had never experienced anything more beautiful.

The dream ended almost as quickly as it formed, and I was violently shaken awake, gazing into the nightmarish eyes of Casimir that I just created. Two whitish, nearly colorless irises gleamed in his face, flashing around the room and swallowing each and every detail. A rough laugh rumbled from the depths of his stomach and shattered the silent air.

"Just as I *imagined*," he yelled, throwing his head back in pride, "*just* as I *imagined*!"

His eyes raked the walls, to the lilac flowers on the table, to the faces of everyone in the room. In a mad stupor, he stumbled to the lantern and turned it so low that every shadow grew. The blue light wavered weakly across his enthusiastic features, swelling over the large bump that was his forehead. He flew to the table, ripped a purple flower out of the vase, and gazed at it. He rubbed his eyes a few times, trying to adjust.

As he released a laugh, the flower crushed in his tight grip, fluttering to the floor in an ugly heap. He approached a mirror that hung on the wall behind the cowering Lucetta, extending a pale finger to stroke the outline of his jaw. His smile grew as he took in his appearance, but disappeared as he spun around to face his son on the floor. Revelin's head was bowed from exhaustion, but his eyes glared piercingly up at his father.

"What a *disappointment*," said Casimir coolly. "It's a shame you're nothing like your sister. Thankfully she's still alive...."

Revelin had been sitting still, unflinchingly, his eyes never leaving Casimir's face. Lucetta had been crouched in the shadows, silently observing the scene. As Casimir's words left his lips, floating into the air and lingering like a ghost made of ice…that silence bled into shock that reflected on each face.

With a burst of courage that stunned everybody, Lucetta sprang from the shadows and advanced on Casimir. Her black tunic fluttered boldly behind her, as if daring someone to restrain it. The tall body swayed elegantly with each step, discharging a sort of intimidation upon Casimir. Her black eyes gleamed fearlessly as she halted just inches in front of her husband.

"You mean to tell me that she is *alive*?" Lucetta snapped, her lips white.

"Lucy…" Casimir whispered, his previously glowing features receding to horror as he realized what he said.

"YOU *LIED* TO ME ABOUT HER *DEATH*?" Lucetta wailed, causing Timoria to cringe.

I slowly sat up, watching as a strange argument I couldn't understand bubbled among Timoria, Lucetta, and Casimir. Damon and Marcus were distracted as well, listening stupidly to Lucetta, their mouths hanging open.

It's time to act, I thought, glancing at my friends, *If I could just sneak over and untie the bonds....*

"Lucy...calm down, let me explain—" Timoria squeaked, stepping to stand beside Casimir with her hands awkwardly held out to try to relax Lucetta.

"WHAT COULD YOU POSSIBLY EXPLAIN, TIMORIA? This is between my *husband* and *me*," Lucetta said sharply, her hands clenched into fists and her muscles stiff.

I locked eye contact with Ali and she nodded enthusiastically, seeming to understand that I wanted to free them. She discreetly jerked her head toward the floor where Timoria seemed to have dropped her knife. I inwardly beamed, thankful that Ali was so observant. Even though chaos was exploding around her, she managed to keep a cool head.

"Well, when you b-became p-pregnant with Revelin," Timoria stuttered, "and he was b-born...and Casimir found out that he was a b-boy—"

"*Out with it, Timoria!*" Lucetta ordered, tears trickling shamelessly down her cheeks.

"When our first child, a girl, was born twenty years ago," Casimir said proudly, no longer cringing from Lucetta, "she was— as you know very well, Lucy—my heir. She is the firstborn, and therefore would become the next leader after I died.

"No matter how much *you* always loved her, *I* always saw her as weak and unfit. We needed a *boy* to become the next leader. So, when Revelin was born, I saw no need to keep our daughter, seeing

140

as she would only get in the way of Revelin's rightful place as leader."

"She was *four years old* when Revelin was born, how could you possibly know that she was *weak* and *unfit*?" Lucetta screeched, the tears now cascading though she still stood rigid with courage.

I crawled off the couch, making as little sound as possible as I approached Nico, Revelin, and Ali and grabbed the knife from the floor. With quiet sawing motions, I began to cut away at Nico's rope. He gazed at me momentarily with admiration, but then his eyes widened in warning. I glanced behind me to see Marcus's blind eyes flicker curiously in my direction. Forced to cut even more slowly so as not to be heard, I soundlessly dragged the knife along the ropes.

"Yes I thought she was weak!" Casimir shouted, "She was just a *girl*!"

"So you just *killed* her?" said Lucetta.

"No…she is *not* dead. Obviously, you must remember how I told you she died in a horrible accident one day when she, Timoria, and I were returning from a journey outside the walls. I told you…what was it?…ah yes, that she was climbing a tree and fell forty feet to her death. I said her body was so destroyed that you wouldn't want to see it, so I buried it before returning to the town.

"But, my dear Lucy, that was a *lie*. You were so devastated ever since, but it was necessary. You see, I'm not entirely coldhearted. I needed some way to get rid of her, but she *is* my daughter. So I took Timoria with me, who has always loved our daughter as if she were her own. While outside the walls, I told Timoria to take our daughter away and hide her. Timoria disagreed, saying she would tell everyone how absurd it all was, but I threatened to kill our daughter if Timoria revealed the secret or messed up one little thing.

"So, Lucy, our *precious* daughter was safely hidden outside the town, out of the way for the past seventeen years. Timoria would go out a few times a week and educate her and bring her some food and necessities. But as our innocent girl grew older, she…changed. Timoria, now if you would explain…" Casimir pressed Timoria to continue.

By the end of Casimir's explanation I almost managed to free Nico, but just as his last rope was a thread away from snapping, my stomach filled with lead at the sound of a shrill hiss.

"Well, your daughter, she—" Timoria began, but Casimir interrupted by pushing her onto the floor as he charged forward to stop me.

"Oh no, you are *not* escaping. Irrational, idiotic child," Casimir bellowed, "Marcus, Damon…how could you've not noticed? Oh, right, because *you're* still *blind*…"

Before I had time to react, Casimir kicked the knife out of my hand and it skidded across the slippery floor only to be stopped by Marcus's foot. I jumped back, but Damon had my hands tied behind my back in a half a second. Nico stood and threw a punch at Damon's face, but it was no use, we were outnumbered.

Nico and I tried to protest, but cloths were fastened over our mouths before a word could be spoken. Damon and Marcus shoved us onto the floor, pushed us against Ali and Revelin, and bound the four of us together tightly with thick rope. My jaw clenched and the dirty cloth dug into my gums.

I was internally writhing with anger at Casimir, the Deceivers, and myself, and I couldn't stop the muffled yells emanating from my mouth.

"SHUT UP!" Damon grunted, a purple bruise forming beneath his eye where Nico had punched him.

However, Damon's command wasn't needed because the pressure of Revelin's hand squeezing my own stifled the cries. He had somehow managed to slip the ropes off his wrists. I glanced at him, seeing my own emotions reflected in his eyes, and understood that he, Nico, and Ali felt the same way. But they couldn't understand the anger I had toward myself, and they never would, because they didn't possess the Gift.

"Now that everyone has finished *whining*," Casimir sneered, "Timoria, finish explaining to Lucy."

Lucetta, who had been watching the struggle with a bowed head and downcast eyes, turned again to Timoria. There was a certain softness to her face that suggested the courage from earlier had faded.

"When my…I mean *your* d-daughter reached the age of seventeen," Timoria continued, her lips quivering, "she changed. She became cold, quiet, and mysterious. When I visited her, she wouldn't speak to me. She wouldn't even look at me.

"And each year after seventeen, she got quieter and stranger. At nineteen, she would approach me without speaking, only staring at me like she knew my darkest secrets. Then just last year, at twenty-one, she vanished.

"Now…d-don't be angry Lucy…but we'd been keeping her in a sort of…house. There was one window on the ceiling, and a door. She had a nice bed in there, and a desk, and all sorts of entertaining things. But I never took her out of the room except for at night. In recent years, she just sat, crouched in the corner, and wouldn't come outside at night. She became almost animal-like: quick and stealthy. I had to keep her hidden, or else Casimir would *kill* her.

"She used to be a beautiful, pleasant child. We would walk around at night and she would always tell me these wonderful stories that she came up with about magical creatures, heroes, and villains. She had such a lovely imagination…but it all disappeared. And the week after her twenty-first birthday, I went to visit her, but she wasn't there."

Timoria finished, and Lucetta was about to speak but Casimir burst into a storm of words.

"And Timoria, if you would've told me about this *change* that my daughter went through, I would've traded her for Revelin immediately! She was becoming *strong* Timoria! She was *powerful*!

"But no, you waited to tell me about my daughter's wondrous

change when it was too late: when she had already escaped. Do you know this *imagination* she had that you speak of? It's *weakness*. But it disappeared, and at the young age of seventeen! She would've been *incredible*, Timoria!" Casimir paused, his eyes alight with a lost dream.

His words reminded me of what Louis had said: *imagination is the key to surviving all that is real*. The light in Casimir's eyes faded, though, as he glared at Revelin.

"Now I'm forced to have this *mess of a son* as my heir. This seventeen-year-old boy who thrives on nothing but hope…for the impossible and the unimportant."

Casimir shook his head in disappointment and gazed at me on the floor, unsure of what to say.

"Revelin hopes for *life*," Lucetta breathed, the courage taking over as she went to stand beside her son, her face glowing with something Casimir would never know, "and I think it's time you release these children. What do you *really* want from the Gift, Casimir? I know you don't want world power. The thing you want is to have your daughter back. And Lilah can't give that to you. Lilah can't give you your daughter's love."

Lucetta's words caused me to flashback to that night when my father told me the story about his dream: the story about how he had dreamed Lucetta to be in love with him, and she was, for a short time. But even the power of the Gift can't overcome a person's true, deep feelings and desires.

"She's just a child, Casimir. You can't force the world on her like this. Stop trying to hide from the truth. Has this truth ever hidden from you?"

As if a ray of scorching sunlight had just burst onto Casimir's face, his expression changed to one of great anger. "WHAT MAKES YOU THINK THAT I WANT MY DAUGHTER'S LOVE?" he roared. "I want the power of the Gift to be mine, and my daughter to be the heir, and for her to be a *powerful ruler*."

Lucetta shook her head in disappointment; persuading Casimir seemed impossible. After a moment's silence, Casimir strutted over to me, his metallic pants and shirt fluttering behind him, as if begging to leave the accursed body. He halted a few feet in front of me.

"Marcus and Damon, take these four and Lucy down to the prison. I need some time to think about what I should make *little Lilah* dream about first. It'll take elaborate planning," Casimir ordered.

The prison only brought one thought to my mind…I would get to see my parents again. I almost happily cooperated when Marcus yanked up the thick rope holding the four of us together. Damon shamelessly grabbed Lucetta's wrists, tied them together, and pushed her out of the room.

"You would *imprison Revelin*? Stop trying to fulfill your father's wishes; he would be ashamed that you treat your own son as an enemy," Lucetta said before Damon silenced her by tying a cloth over her mouth.

My last sight of Casimir was of his pacing the room, so deep in thought that he wouldn't even pause to reply to Lucetta, or blink his eyes. Timoria remained in the room with him, her face downcast. Marcus shoved Revelin, Nico, Ali, and me out of the room and closed the door behind him. Because we were tied together, we had to step gingerly down the silver staircase so that we wouldn't fall, which only angered Marcus. I watched Lucetta in front of us with pity settled in my stomach as Damon harshly dragged her by the elbow toward one of the doors guarded by a Deceiver.

"Prisoners," Damon grunted.

The hook-nosed Deceiver guarding the door opened it and stepped aside. A musty, dank draft of air billowed from the darkness beyond the door. Marcus pushed the four of us toward the door and down a long staircase, followed by Lucetta and Damon.

There were no lights, so we fumbled blindly down the steps. Because my feet were bare, I noticed that the floor was no longer metal, but slippery stone. It felt as if we were going down a hundred steps, the air getting colder every second. The only thing that I could think of was seeing my parents again, and as we reached the bottom of the staircase, I could have smiled if it weren't for the situation we were in.

The first thing I spotted was my mother and father sitting on a large stone against the wall of a cell. They appeared sick, thin, and tired, but they were alive. And beside them were no other than Mr. and Mrs. Aljoy, Nico's parents.

The cell was small, a little bigger than my room at home, and tightly compressed metal bars, which were impossible to slip through, surrounded it. About five Deceivers, two of whom weren't blind, paced around the cell wielding metal nightsticks. A single candle burned in a lantern against the wall in the cell, and I realized that it was the lantern I saw when Revelin and I tried to free the prisoners.

"Lilah," my mother whispered, a tear of joy streaking down her cheek as she and my father stood and ran toward me. The bars stopped them, and they stood there with their faces pressed against the metal, staring at me.

Marcus opened the cell door and Lucetta, Revelin, Nico, Ali, and I were forced into it. The door closed and locked with a *clink* and Damon returned up the staircase with Marcus on his heels. Mr. and Mrs. Aljoy and my parents immediately dashed toward us, untying the cloths and ropes. My father's eyes roamed to Lucetta, his cheeks blushing madly, but she returned the look with a frown.

"Mom, Dad, Nico, Regina, *everyone*…I should've…this is all my fault—" I said tightly as soon as the cloth was removed from my mouth. I was interrupted, however, when eight people embraced me tightly, many arms squeezing me.

"You've been so brave, sweetie," my mother said.

"We're just glad you're alright," my father sighed.

"You really showed my dad. He was *so* angry," Revelin grinned into my shoulder.

"It's not your fault, Lilah. Without you, my sisters and brothers would still be trapped in this prison," Ali said, her arms wrapped around my waist.

"Yeah, woo, brilliant. But next time, try to dream up a Porsche or something, like the one Louis drew a picture of. I'd like one of those," Nico said with a wink.

Everyone broke away from the hug and stared at him, eyebrows raised.

"I'm just kidding," Nico said quickly, blushing.

"Who is this *Portia*? Louis *drew a picture* of her? Young man, if I find out Louis's been influencing you badly or you've been *anywhere* near a girl—" Regina roared.

"Porsche, not Portia. It's a *car*, mom. Not a *girl*," Nico replied, his entire face turning red.

For what seemed like ages since it last happened, we laughed, the pleasant sound echoing through the prison. But a sound of metal clanking against metal made us fall silent. A Deceiver was dragging her nightstick against the bars of the cell, her thin lips curled in a snarl.

"Stop *LAUGHING*!" she shrieked, hitting the metal bars so hard that the entire cell rattled.

The light mood was executed as if it had never happened. As everyone around me settled in to the cell, some nestling down to sleep on the paper-thin, brown and gray blankets in the corner of the room, and some talking to each other, only one thought flooded my mind.

Really, I was just a slave waiting for orders…waiting for Casimir to decide what he wanted me to dream…waiting for the moment when I would have to leave my friends and family behind and fulfill the wishes of a crazed man.

11 The Heir's Message

The air in the cell had warmed considerably, and after what seemed like four weeks, I guessed that it was the middle of warm weather. My parents were getting weaker and Revelin and I bickered constantly. My father distanced himself from Lucetta, who lingered around the door of the cell, not speaking with anyone, lost in her own thoughts about her daughter. No matter how hard we tried, nobody could get any more information out of her, and Revelin was still mulling over the fact that his older sister was alive.

Everyone had lost track of what time of day it was, since there were no windows or views of the outside. We tried multiple times to get through the secret passage under the stone, but the Deceivers had found it and clogged it with heavy rocks and dirt. We slept restlessly, and the shadows beneath my eyes were worse than ever because I didn't sleep...I dreaded dreaming. Without the Dream-Catcher, the usual threat of accidental destructive dreams had returned, and my father constantly warned me to sleep carefully. That was the least of the issues, though…all I could do was wonder when Casimir would finish devising his plans.

Nico, Ali, and I were huddled in the corner of the cell, discussing anything besides Casimir. The adults, except for Lucetta, were sitting in the center, and my father seemed to be telling them the history of the Gift—and all its details—in a hushed voice.

"I wonder what Louis is doing right now," Ali said absentmindedly, her cheeks pale from lack of sunlight. "I wonder if he knows we're in here. And Henry, Andrew, Alf, Tina, and Tara…."

"I'm sure they're all fine, Ali," I said reassuringly. "How long d'you think we've been in here? It feels like months."

Nico shifted uncomfortably; he, too, was paler and overly attentive from lack of sleep. From the front of the cell, Revelin ambled over to us, looking not nearly as exhausted as the rest of us.

"The sun set three hours ago, so it's night. And it's been nearly four weeks. It's almost December," he said with an air of impatience. However, nobody really knew what that meant, except that it was somewhere near the middle of warm weather because of how hot it was. Specific dates were something that no one recognized.

"How d'you know?" Nico asked.

Revelin joined our circle, planting himself between me and

Ali. He leaned back against the bars of the cell, folding his arms behind his head and releasing a long breath.

"Jackson, that Deceiver over there, just told me. I've known him for my entire life; he's been living here ever since I was born. That doesn't change anything though—he still hates my guts, just like the rest of them," he said, pointing to a Deceiver with shadowy skin and short silver hair that was pacing around.

"Wouldn't you *rather* be hated by the Deceivers? I wouldn't want to be liked by something so *foul*," Ali said. Nico's eyes widened in surprise. The absence of fresh air must have been getting to her, because she had never said anything that harsh before. Sadly, though, I agreed with her.

"Yeah, I guess so," Revelin replied offhandedly, his glowing eyes flickering over every face in the room. He sighed with a sudden annoyance. "Lilah, it's *pointless* for us to sit here any longer. *Why* haven't you dreamed us out yet?"

"You shouldn't ask me things regarding the Gift. It's too complex to explain," I said.

"Why aren't you answering my question?" he pressed.

"Why are you questioning my answer?" I said.

Nico snorted.

"Stop, enough *bickering*," Ali pleaded. "You've been at it for days now."

"You know what, Revelin? Maybe Timoria was right about your loving Lilah. You try to get her attention by being difficult all the time," Nico snapped.

"Timoria doesn't know *anything* about me," he chuckled deeply. "The only reason why I tried to keep Lilah away from my father was because of the *Gift*. I didn't want to think about the awful things he would do if he got her."

"Well then leave her alone! Stop *bothering* her! Is it that hard to be *nice* for once?" Nico spat, straightening his posture so as to look directly at Revelin.

"I don't take orders from anyone," Revelin sneered.

"I thought you two were supposed to be *friends*!" Ali reminded them.

Nico glanced at her and stopped fuming; Revelin stood and walked away, muttering to himself, and I sighed deeply, trying to ward off the annoyance.

A comfortable silence settled as the adults retired to sit against the back wall. Lucetta stood, facing the stairs that led up and out of the prison, her face pressed against the metal bars that caged her in. Her black hair, tumbling in thick waves down to her elbows, was tangled and dry. She wouldn't speak to anyone except Revelin unless it was absolutely necessary.

I stood drowsily and stretched, my stomach feeling empty from an evening meal of a few pieces of bread. Nearing the door of the cell, I tapped the shoulder of the Deceiver named Jackson who was guarding it and he turned to unlock it. After locking the door again, he grabbed my wrist and prepared to lead me to the bathroom which was down a narrow corridor beside the cell. I didn't actually need to use the bathroom…it was just impossible to sit still behind the bars.

As his cold fingers closed around my arm and he blinked his non-blind eyes, a whistling sound pierced the air so faint that I took no notice of it, thinking my ears were deceiving me. Before Jackson could even flinch, something that looked like a black needle shot through the air from the direction of the staircase and sank into the side of his neck.

I easily leaped away from Jackson's grip as he stepped backwards, his eyes bulging. His hand flew up to where the needle had punctured him, and he winced horribly as he yanked out a five-inch, thin black dart.

Another dart flew through the air, but I was too distracted to see who its target was. Jackson stared at the staircase, but nobody was there. The entire room had fallen silent except for strange whimpers sounding from the cell.

The black dart slipped from Jackson's fingers, clattering to the stone floor. His black eyes rolled back in his head, his knees buckled, and he crumpled to the floor. Within half a minute, his breathing had stopped completely.

"What's going on? What did you *do*?" hissed a non-blind woman Deceiver as she flung herself onto the floor and felt Jackson's pulse. "He's *dead*! YOU KILLED HIM!"

She lashed out, knocking me down and pinning me to the floor. I tried unsuccessfully to free myself as she drew out a nasty curved knife, bringing it dangerously close to my neck. From the corner of my eye, I could see everyone in the cell huddled in a circle, staring at something on the floor. The other Deceivers rushed to the woman's side, all drawing out their own knife.

"You don't understand. Look, on the floor over there…someone shot a dart at his neck," I said. My heart was pounding as the woman's knife inched closer to my neck. I glanced at the cell again and saw Revelin kneeling on the floor, his body convulsing. My blood went cold as I realized the other dart had hit him.

"You *lie!*" shrieked the woman stupidly, not even turning to look if there was a dart.

Just as her curved knife grazed my skin, a long, deep yell rumbled down the staircase and filled the prison. All heads turned to face the stone steps which seemed to be shaking as somebody ran down and stumbled into the room. The woman who had been pinning me to the floor suddenly stood up as Casimir emerged. He stood rigidly at the foot of the stairs, the Dream-Catcher gleaming against his chest.

My stomach dropped as I thought he must have come down to retrieve me, and that his elaborate plans for my dreams were complete. His face was grim and furious, however, not excited. I pulled myself into a sitting position, forcing myself not to look at Revelin. He couldn't be dead: I wouldn't believe it.

I watched Casimir storm forward and kneel to the dead Jackson, and then carefully pick up the black dart. His eyes swallowed each detail, from the thin, crooked black feathers on one end to the incredibly sharp metal tip. I could just make out the smallest letter C carved into the metal.

"HOW COULD THIS BE HAPPENING? WHY WOULD SHE DO THIS?" Casimir bellowed, veins throbbing on his neck. His anger morphed quickly, though, into a look of disturbing admiration. "No, this is good. This is *very* good…look at how powerful she is…but there's no way I'll give it to her. There's no way…."

Casimir was shaken out of a daze as he glanced at me on the floor. "WHAT IS SHE DOING OUT OF THE CELL?" he yelled.

The woman Deceiver cringed and then grabbed me, dragging me into the cell and locking the door again behind me. Casimir's gaze was suddenly locked onto something I couldn't see, and I turned when I noticed how silent the room had become. Lying there on the cold floor, somewhat hidden by the people huddled around her, was Lucetta, a dart planted in her neck.

Revelin wasn't shaking because he was hit with the other dart; he was shaking because his mother was dead.

All of the air had somehow escaped my lungs as I unconsciously walked over to Lucetta, kneeling beside her head which rested lifelessly against the stone floor. My vision was blurred as I tugged the dart from her neck, watching as Revelin sat curled over his mother's body as if protecting it, his chest heaving. Ali kneeled beside me, trying to feel the pulse on Lucetta's neck and paling as she realized all life had already vanished. Nico and all the others in the cell were overcome with shock.

"What kind of *heartless*, *worthless* monster—" I shouted,

springing up and flying toward the cell door. I didn't try to hide my face as angry tears streaked my cheeks; and as I neared Casimir, he took a few steps back. He didn't seem too distressed over his wife's death, but his face was crumpled in a scowl.

Anger clouding my mind, I viciously tried to grab Casimir through the bars, even though I knew he wasn't the murderer. I could hear Revelin sobbing quietly behind me, but a second later, he joined me and hurtled himself at Casimir, his mouth hanging open as if in a silent scream.

"WHAT DID YOU DO TO HER?" Revelin shrieked.

Out of the corner of my eye, I saw Nico grab Revelin around the waist, attempting to restrain him. After a few more moments of lashing out violently, Revelin sank to his knees, his blood-shot eyes wide and his jaw clamped tightly. I went to stand beside Nico, placing a hand on his shoulder, thanking him.

"*I* did nothing. It was my daughter, of course," Casimir admitted, casting Revelin a snarl, his face still crumpled. "Nobody saw her. Nobody heard her. I was sitting in my room, not paying attention, and when I stood up, Timoria was slumped against the wall…*dead*. One of the same darts that killed Jackson was lodged in her neck. Poison, I'm guessing…*so* intelligent. My daughter is so *intelligent*. But she's cunning, too…she left a note. She didn't just kill for fun."

Revelin was disturbingly silent as he sat in a daze, his cheeks still wet from tears. His arms hung limply at his sides as he stared at his father.

Casimir's mood darkened as he retrieved a small piece of dirty paper from his pocket. He unfolded it and made a non-blind Deceiver read it aloud, because even though Casimir was now able to see, he was never taught to read.

"Do you remember seventeen years ago," the fearful Deceiver began to read, "as you led me out of the town, and locked me in a house to keep me hidden? All those years you pretended I was dead, abandoning me to be mothered by Timoria? I can remember the excitement in your voice as you told me you had a new child, a son. However, your son grew up to be the opposite of what you had hoped for. He grew up to be the weakling you thought I was.

"In those years you hid me away, I was angry for a while. But just last year when I escaped, I realized that in those years you isolated me, you were giving me a chance to become better. And I have, father. I've improved. And now that you've captured the girl with the Gift, together we could use her for the greatest things.

"I'm sorry that those who suffered a surprising death were dear to you; they were also dear to me. But they were blocking our way to success, father. The deaths tonight were significant. Timoria knew too much about me and my secret, and she had to be eliminated. Jackson's death was the only one that was unnecessary; he just happened to be in my line of fire of Lucetta. The death of Lucetta will be the toughest for you to understand.

"You see, Revelin is currently a threat. He is stubborn, relentless, and daring; and the townspeople believe he is the rightful heir. His mother's death will rot him from the inside out, making him vulnerable and submissive. Now, when I return to take my place as your heir, there is no threat of Revelin's rejecting or starting a rebellion. Why, you might ask, didn't I just kill Revelin? Simply because that would destroy the townspeople. They would be angry and frightened. It is safer to diminish hope instead of dousing it.

"I cherish the memories I have of you, father, and hope each day to be with you again. I can clearly remember your great strength and acute reasoning.

"Tomorrow, when the sun sets, call your townspeople to a gathering. Bring the girl with the Gift, her friends, and Revelin. Show all the townspeople how weak your son is, and how unfit he is to rule. Then, when the moment is right, I will appear. You will explain that I'm the rightful heir, and we'll return to the palace where we can live together. Signed, your daughter Cyra." The Deceiver handed the note back to Casimir, his fingers shaking. Cyra was the name of the rightful heir, and that was why a letter C was carved into the dart. All these years, and hardly anyone knew a *girl* was the great Deceiver's heir.

"Yes, my daughter has *returned*," Casimir said, averting his eyes from his dead wife. "The note was nailed to the door of my room with yet another poison dart. How she managed it all without being seen or heard, I'll never know. Clever girl…but she won't get the Gift. I want all of you," he motioned to the Deceivers, "to guard the entrance to the prison. The staircase's the only way down here, and I'm keeping every last Deceiver on watch. If a soul passes the first step, kill them. My daughter might try to take Lilah during the night, and that can't happen. I don't fear Lilah's dreams right now; she isn't capable of dreaming anything devastating with so little experience. And tomorrow when we bring the Gift to the gathering, Lilah must also be heavily guarded."

With a deprecating glance at his son and a sickly frown at his dead wife, Casimir turned and glided up the staircase, followed closely by all the Deceivers. A door slammed in the distance, and we were alone. I withdrew from the bars of the cell, wanting more than anything not to turn around and face something I had never seen before. Death.

Revelin approached Lucetta and kneeled beside her again, his face white as a bone and lacking emotion. I willed myself to turn and as I stared at the peaceful, lifeless face on the floor, a thought nagged continually at the back of my mind: Why not just dream Lucetta back to life?

Ali, Nico, and I stood beside each other, unsure of what to do besides gaze at the wilted beauty who lay gracefully upon the stone floor. Mr. Aljoy and Regina remained silent, my mother's eyes were shut, and my father's face was drained as if something very dear to him was stolen away. My mother was clueless of his past love, clueless of his *first* love. Unable to stand it any longer, I grabbed Revelin's arm and forced him onto his feet, and he didn't object, which was frightening.

"Stop...d-don't cry," I said. "I—I can dream her back to life...I know I can. It'd be so easy. Just give me a minute to fall asleep—"

"No, Lilah," my father ordered. He left my mother's side and placed his hands on my shoulders. His forehead was wrinkled with grief. "Listen to me. Bringing a soul back to a body is one of the few things that you must *never* dream. Do you know where a soul goes after a person dies?"

"No," I said quietly. "Do you?"

"Of course not. But you see, that's how it's supposed to be. If we knew, there would be no more mystery. There would be no more guessing. There would be no more reason for faith. Just as a fish belongs in water and not on land, a free soul belongs in the Unknown. And if Lucetta's soul is brought back, she would be able to *tell* us where a soul goes after death. The Unknown would become the known. And you can't mess with things like that, Lilah. Just as you can't mess with genuine love."

Every eye in the cell was glued to my father, absorbing his words, some not quite sure what he was saying and others understanding completely. I nodded at him, remembering how he had tried to make Lucetta love him but found it was impossible. He released my shoulders, some of the depression in the room dissipating. Revelin stared at his mother with the strongest hurt in his eyes, his chest compressing as if exhaling his final breath.

"Don't let this destroy you, Revelin," Ali said as she, Nico, and I placed our hands supportively on his shoulders.

"You're stronger than this. You're stronger than Cyra," Nico encouraged.

"Lucetta didn't die in vain. All people pass eventually, some sooner than others. But it seems those whom you love the most, die the soonest. And why? Because they are the ones you expect to live the longest," my father whispered, not quite sure what he was trying to say.

Tears still trickled shamelessly along Revelin's cheeks, and his face was crumpled sourly. But his courage wasn't completely doused. "If you can't bring her back to life," he said tightly, "can you bury her body somewhere peaceful? I can't just leave her down here where it's cold and dark."

My father nodded in approval and I relaxed onto one of the blankets, focusing on Lucetta. The cell was silent as I closed my eyes and pictured her elegant face at peace beneath the soft earth of a forest somewhere far away. I was lulled into a light sleep, the vivid colors of my dream seeming so real, as honey-like ribbons of sunlight dripped through the trees and warmed the ground above where Lucetta lay. Red and blue birds sang her name over and over again; their cheerful chirps awakened the plants, and a bed of wildflowers bloomed above Lucetta, forever preserving her beauty. The sky was a clear, vibrant blue and no shadows existed. Even in my sleep, I could feel the breeze in the forest…it was almost real enough for *me* to actually be there….

I was awoken by the sound of loud gasps echoing through the cell. Startled, I shot out of the bed, rubbing my eyes. Everyone was circled around the spot where Lucetta had died, gazing at the floor. As I peered past their feet, I could see a single white wildflower—

which had replaced Lucetta's body—sprouting from a crack in the stone. Each face except for Revelin's was stretched into a gentle smile.

"You did it, Lilah," Nico said.

"So I did," I sighed, relieved and happy. "What did it look like when…when her body left? Did it…levitate out of the room?" I asked carefully, unable to contain my curiosity. Everyone except for Revelin laughed softly.

"No. We were watching her, and suddenly it was like her body was made of mist, evaporating from the floor. It was beautiful, really," Regina said delicately. My mother smiled, but my father's eyes, however, lingered longingly on the floor near the wildflower. I wasn't aware of how long I had been asleep, but it must have been long enough for everyone to return to their usual states— everyone except for my father and Revelin.

As drowsiness settled, people retired to the blankets. I stayed awake, though, sitting on the floor beside the wildflower and lost in thought. The candlelight from the lantern on the wall twinkled dimly on the glossy white petals of the flower, making it appear on fire. Long after I thought everyone had fallen asleep, a rustling sound came from behind me and my father gradually appeared, sitting across from me.

Now that I took the time to look at him, I realized that he had lost a significant amount of weight. The belt around his waist had half-a-foot or so of room between the metal and his stomach. He sat with his arms crossed over his knees, and his back was hunched with fatigue. When he lifted his eyes to look at me, they looked so similar to mine with the baggy shadows underneath.

"He'll be alright. He's a good kid, you know," he said mostly to himself, glancing at the corner of the cell where Revelin was fast asleep. "And *wise*, too...at least more so than I when I was his age."

"I'm *not* the right person for the Gift, Dad. I don't want it," I said suddenly. My thoughts had to be revealed to him...there was no reason to hide them. And who better to share them with than the man who had the Gift before me?

"Lilah," he sighed, momentarily closing his eyes, "why do you tell yourself things like this?"

"Because how am I any different from Andrew, Ali, Revelin, or Nico? There's nothing that makes *me* so worthy of the Gift. If you truly think about it, Dad, you'll see that there are so many others who *should* have it."

"Do you know those stories you always tell to Andrew," he said calmly, "the ones full of treacherous tasks, danger, and impossible journeys? Usually in your stories, there is one character who stands out from the rest: the person who makes everything better in the end. But rarely does Andrew realize that that character—the hero—is *chosen* by *you*: the storyteller. There is a great difference between those who are *chosen* to be the hero and those who simply *are* the hero."

"But aren't we all the heroes of our own stories? Nobody in their right mind would *want* to be a villain."

"Yes, but is *everyone* in their right mind?"

"Who's to say anybody is? Who's to judge the difference between a wrong and right mind?"

My father grinned. "I fear that I don't have an answer for everything, Lilah. Your questions are a bit too mystifying for me.

"Many people are blessed with things that they do not deserve. Some have great talents, wealth, or intelligence, yet they lack some of the most important qualities of all: wisdom and humility. And for your age, you have a great deal of both. You believe that the Gift shouldn't belong to you because you expect too much of yourself. Remember your age. Remember you're just fifteen."

"Dad, if you think these things of me, why not encourage me to use the Gift? Do you know how simple it would be for me to just dream none of this ever happened? I could dream that the wall was never built around the town, or the Deceivers and Casimir no longer existed. I could dream the Gift would leave me and never come back to anyone—"

As to silence me, my father shook his head vigorously. "Altering things that have already happened is something else that you *must* avoid. If you dream the Deceivers never existed, Revelin wouldn't've been born. If you dreamed the wall was never built, I may have never met your mother and…generations would be lost. Memories would be changed.

"However, dreaming that the Gift would leave you is something I've tried before. It's one of the only things that's impossible for you, Lilah. It simply doesn't work. One night long ago, when I was a little older than you are, I began to hate the Gift. I couldn't sleep without fear…I couldn't close my eyes without hoping I wouldn't think about death and destruction—much like you have to do every night…except *you* have more tolerance. So naturally, I tried to get rid of the Gift. I dreamed that it left me and would never return to anyone. But what I didn't realize is that the Gift was *part of me*. It would be like trying to remove an aspect of someone's personality.

"The dream worked similarly to the time…" he lowered his voice and glanced at my sleeping mother, "when I tried to make Lucetta love me. It was true for a few weeks or so…the Gift was actually *gone* for a few weeks. But then, like Lucetta's dislike for me, it came back even stronger. There are so many things that we will never know, Lilah. There are so many mysteries that our ancestors left, and that we will never solve."

"Then we have to at least try to live as they did, be as meek and humble as they were," I said.

"Yes, Lilah. I think you finally understand," my father grinned. "But Casimir doesn't. He doesn't see the importance of humility, at least not right now. He's blinded by his own greed. He acts brave and confident, but really he's fearful. He uses a false arrogant confidence to reassure himself."

I nodded and we didn't speak for a few minutes. "Dad, why did Lucetta marry Casimir?" I asked, still staring at the flower and imagining Lucetta's body turning into mist as it disappeared.

Even in the darkness, I could see his cheeks flush pink with surprise. "Well…that's a very good question. And if you knew Lucetta when you were my age, you would see your question also has quite an obvious answer. You know very well how beautiful she was, and I told you how alluring she was. She had such charm. And Casimir, being the leader's heir, could have *nearly anything* he asked for. So Lucetta was forced to marry him."

I tried to imagine Casimir in a suit, waiting for Lucetta to walk up to him in her white dress, like some of the weddings I had seen in Delvadar Alley before. The weddings were never extravagant, but I could almost always tell the couple genuinely loved each other. Casimir's wedding must have been quite the opposite.

"She was awfully courageous to live with him as a husband. I buried her somewhere so beautiful, Dad…in a forest under a bed of wildflowers, somewhere where the sun never ceases to shine. But where, Dad? Where are these places? Louis was talking to me about continents. D'you know which one we're on? Didn't your grandfather know, and then tell your father, and then tell you?" I asked.

"You're so curious that it's sometimes frightening," my father said, making me smile. "But I can't speak about those things. I-I told you that Casimir will kill anyone who talks about it."

"But Louis talks about it. And why doesn't Casimir allow anyone to speak of it?"

"Louis is frightfully daring, and the Deceivers don't really care because they know he's forgotten all about it. And Casimir doesn't allow it because he believes it leads to curiosity and an increase in people's desire to escape. Deceivers are always watching. But I'll at least tell you that no, I'm not exactly sure where we are. My father told me a complicated story about it once, but now isn't the time to tell it to you."

Unable to think of another way to wheedle anything out of him, I simply nodded. The others in the cell, though clearly asleep, rustled restlessly. My father looked as if he were about to stand and return to sleep, but there was still another question burning in my mind.

"Dad, wait," I said quickly, causing him to remain sitting. "Do you know anything about…have you ever before heard of—"

"Cyra?" he interrupted, finishing my sentence. I nodded and he sighed deeply. "Yes, every townsperson was told about Cyra's supposed death. We all knew her as a child; she was kindhearted, bold, and had such a free spirit. She was the most *beautiful* girl that anyone had ever seen, and charming just like her mother. We all thought it was somewhat suspicious that Cyra had 'died' the same week that Revelin was born, but we accepted it nonetheless. It was a devastating time; and in return, naturally, everyone disliked Revelin. That's why the kids in the town constantly told you bad things about him, because he was born into a bad reputation. Everybody wanted Cyra to be the leader's heir, and in their mind, Revelin ruined that."

"That's unfair to Revelin…nobody even gave him a chance to show his good qualities. Well…I guess that *I* never really gave him a chance either," I said with a guilty toss of my stomach. "But how could somebody so wonderful like Cyra turn into somebody cruel enough to kill her mother…to kill at all?"

My father nodded proudly when he heard the guilt in my voice over never giving Revelin a chance. His pride faltered, though, when he thought of Cyra again. "She was locked in a room for nearly twenty-one years…but ultimately, I don't know what could've brought such a disturbing change in her personality. And Lilah, sometimes those who seem the most innocent on the outside are the most corrupt on the inside. Goodnight now," he said, standing and ruffling my hair as he used to when I was younger. "Try to get some sleep. I don't know what's going to happen at the gathering but we can talk about it more tomorrow."

"Goodnight Dad," I said with a small smile as he settled back onto a blanket.

I remained on the floor for a few more minutes, listening to the rhythmic sounds of quiet breathing as everyone slept, watching a beetle as it climbed up the stem of the wildflower, struggling to reach the white blossom.

As I fell into a dreamless sleep, the only thing that crossed my thoughts like cracks of lightning in the night was the sound of Cyra's poisonous darts slicing through the air, searching for a new target, haunting the most hidden corners of my mind.

12 The Presentation

"No, Nico…listen to me," I said, grabbing his wrist as we stood alone in a corner of the cell. After placing it in his hand, I closed his fingers around the one thing that could help us. "This needs to be quick. We can't do *anything* wrong, or they'll suspect us. Cyra's going to reclaim her place as heir, and then we need to act at exactly the right time. We can't tell my parents, Ali, Revelin, or anyone else because their reactions won't be genuine enough."

Nico swallowed and his forehead crinkled. "I can't do it, Lilah. Why would you choose me? I'm not *special* like you. I'm not *rebellious* like Revelin. I'm not *quick-witted* like Ali."

"You might not be those things, but Nico, *you* can make *anybody* believe what you say is true."

"You actually think so?" he asked, unconvinced.

"I really do."

"But Cyra's going to attack! D'you really think she's going to make an *ordinary* entrance? If she killed those three people without hesitation…I don't want to think about what she'll do at the gathering." His brown eyes flashed nervously. "I c-can't let you...l-leave my sight like the last time the Deceivers captured me."

The memory flickered across my mind of Nico's hand slipping from mine as Revelin carried me away from a colliding crowd of townspeople and Deceivers. He blushed furiously and I shook my head impatiently.

"That's not going to happen this time!" I said too loudly, glancing at the front of the cell where the others were eating breakfast. Luckily nobody had heard me. "C'mon, we can do this. I… t-trust…you, Nico," I stuttered quietly, a blush creeping along my neck.

He turned to walk over to the food and nodded tensely. "I'll do my best." Ali must have seen the conversation because she tossed various looks of curiosity at me and Nico.

Pale, cracked, and dry, many lips parted as stale bread entered our mouths. Some earthy water and a few pieces of chicken were divided, and breakfast passed without a word from anyone; even Regina managed to be silent. Revelin avoided everything, sitting with his face pressed against the bars, his upper lip twitching occasionally. Most of the anger had left him overnight, but he remained expressionless…his insides twisting with the feelings he kept hidden.

My father's eyes, red and lifeless, showed that he hadn't gotten any sleep. Sometimes I wondered how my mother could possibly be unaware that he had loved Lucetta so dearly, but as I looked at her sitting beside my father, I finally understood.

She was watching him eat, her lips curved into a soft, sympathetic smile, and her eyes were dark with knowledge. She *knew* that my father had loved Lucetta, but she never told anyone! She pretended to be oblivious because she knew that my father already struggled with enough guilt. I focused on the food again, acting as if I hadn't just found my mother's deepest secret.

"*YOU IDIOTS*! Yes I told you not to let *anyone* into the cell, but it's *ME*! Let me pass." Yelling echoed down the staircase and I recognized Casimir's voice, strained and heavy as if he had been upset.

Within seconds he was storming down the stairs, stumbling on the last step. Two Deceivers had followed him, but he ordered them to return to their duties. The Dream-Catcher, bright and mystifying, dangled loosely around his neck, but still it was almost as if the curse had returned. He didn't even seem to notice that Lucetta's body was gone.

"Everyone, listen to me," he said, spit flying through his teeth as he stood a few feet away from the cell.

All eyes turned to him, nobody having the motivation to speak or protest. Even Revelin lifted his eyes, which were like two stones in his face.

"Tonight I will be reclaiming my daughter as the *rightful* heir," he said, a forced smile creeping along his lips. "If you fail to keep *secret* the murders that she committed, or if you say anything *foul* about her, then understand that your time in this prison will never end.

"Michael and Regina Aljoy, Aaron and Jane Keeper," he said, pointing to them as he spoke their names, "you will be able to go home to your families tonight before the gathering, if you cooperate. I don't need you anymore. As for the others, disobey me and your siblings will disappear."

Casimir's grin widened as he walked nearer to the corner of the cell where I stood. "As for you…pretty, pretty girl…" he smirked, causing my teeth to clench.

Revelin's back stiffened. Nico huffed loudly.

Casimir simply chuckled and continued, "I've been thinking, day and night…devising an elaborate plan for your dream. There's one minor detail I must discuss with my daughter, but be prepared for tonight, when the moon is high in the sky. Then you will dream.

"*TONIGHT!*" He shouted, thrusting his fists in the air with triumph. "*Tonight* I will once again have my proper heir standing beside me. Tonight I will have everything I want in this *world*…and even beyond it. Tonight…I'll fulfill my father's wishes." He tripped once again on the last step as he walked up the stairs, muttering happily to himself.

Once all was silent again, I turned to find everyone staring at me as if expecting a miracle, as if I could fix the entire situation with the blink of an eye; as if I were their last hope.

"Dad, I have to *try*," I said quietly.

My father winced as everyone turned to stare at him. He

stepped forward so that we faced each other in the center. "Try *what*, Lilah?! Dream that we're all safe outside of the walls, away from Casimir? Then what about the rest of the townspeople? Would you leave them here to suffer under the anger of Casimir? You can't dream each and every townsperson safe and out of the walls, especially when you have *no idea* what the world *looks like* outside of the walls.

"Or maybe you want to try to make Casimir and the Deceivers disappear. But then *Revelin would die*! He would've never existed! Even the Deceivers don't deserve to be killed. I've seen a rebellious spark—just like Revelin has—in some of them. They have hearts too. You can't use the Gift to kill, Lilah. It should be used for *good* purposes." He took a deep breath and tried to lower his voice. "It's all too complicated. No matter what you dream, there will always be bad consequences."

"So I'm supposed to sit and watch all of this happen, when I'm very capable of stopping it? I'm supposed to let all of you continue to live like this, and be trapped in this town because of *me* and the *Gift*?" I said.

"YES! You have to!" he yelled. "You've always had trouble with seeing the outcomes and consequences of things, Lilah. You're too *impulsive*. For once, *please*, try to think ahead. Think of the future. I know you don't trust very easily…but you *must* trust me on this. Remember, I had the Gift before you."

Finally his reasoning was sinking into me, and after seeing all the people around me that I loved silently agreeing with my father,

I understood how ignorantly I had been acting. Everything that I wanted to dream would have some negative result, and it wasn't worth risking lives for. Feeling defeated, I nodded and went to a corner, isolating myself from the others. I could finally understand why Revelin wanted to be alone.

Within the next few hours, both Nico and Ali tried to talk to me, but I was non-responsive. The plan I had formed with Nico was racing through my mind, making me search for flaws, picking through the details. I could never tell what time of day it was because of the lack of windows, but I was sure it was nearing sunset. A few Deceivers came down to clean us and give us fresh clothes, so as to make us "presentable" for Cyra. Once they left the cell again, I decided it was time to move.

The air seemed to part as if giving me a clear path as I stood from the corner and walked to Revelin. Immediately Ali noticed and opened her mouth to speak, but turned away as she realized that I needed privacy. Everyone else followed her example, hoping that maybe I could bring Revelin to the surface.

He was sitting in the farthest corner of the cell, his back resting against the stone wall and facing the staircase. His legs were sprawled out in front of him and his arms hung limply against his sides. As I sat beside him, sure to keep a distance, I said nothing, but stared at him. He rotated his head to look at me, not showing any signs of interest in conversation. After a minute of silence and staring each other down, he finally spoke.

"I know what you're going to ask," he said tiredly, "and I

can't do it. You don't know how much everyone already loves her."

"No, there's nothing you can do to influence the townspeople that you're a better ruler than Cyra. But you don't *need* to," I said.

For the first time in a while, an emotion sprouted on his face. "What do you mean?" he asked confusedly.

"Nico and I made a plan," I said, lowering my voice. "I can't tell you anything about it, but there is one thing I need you to do in order for it to work."

"Lilah...don't tell me you're going to try to escape...."

I opened my mouth to reply, but Casimir's voice cracked like electricity down the staircase and into the cell. "I DON'T CARE IF YOU HAVEN'T EATEN IN TWO DAYS. GO DOWN THERE AND GET THE ELDERLY ONES! We don't need them anymore."

I watched as a bony Deceiver scuttled down the stairs and glanced nervously behind him. He unlocked the cell door. "Alright, all ya old gimps, come out! It's time for ya to go home."

Mr. and Mrs. Aljoy easily said goodbye to Nico, promising that Casimir would let him go home after the gathering. After all, *I* was the only one that Casimir wanted to keep. My parents led me to a corner, both wringing their hands with worry. It must not have settled in their minds until right then that I would be locked away from their sight for who knew how long. They were too caught up in thinking about Cyra and the gathering.

"It's g-going to be okay, Lilah...we'll find a way to g-get you out of here b-before Casimir makes you dream. There has to be some way…I-I can—" my father stuttered, breathing heavily.

"NO, AARON! We'll get her out *tonight*, before the gathering…we'll hide her away. It's okay Lilah, don't worry at all. Casimir isn't actually going to make you dream," my mother lied to herself.

I didn't know what to say…there wasn't anything I *could* say. "I love you both; *please* watch out for Andrew."

"OUT! NOW!" the bony Deceiver shrieked, pretending not to have heard our conversation and pointing his nightstick at my parents.

Reluctantly they left the cell, calling back to me as they disappeared up the staircase behind Mr. and Mrs. Aljoy. The Deceiver locked the cell again and threatened to hit them if they didn't stop talking. I exhaled a breath, feeling it float through the air and leave with my parents. It was more comforting to know they would be with Andrew, than standing beside me. When I turned, expecting to see Ali and Nico sitting in one corner and Revelin in another, I was shocked to see the three of them standing in the center, waiting for me to join them. Revelin was still aloof, but he gazed forward with such intensity that I knew he was willing to help.

"*Finally*…" Nico said with a sigh. Suddenly he shook his head, making his hair stand up in unbelievable angles, un-tucked his shirt from his shorts, and sprinted in a circle around the inside of the cell twice, nearly slipping on a patch of dirt. "TRY AND

STOP ME, MUM! Oh that's right, *you can't*!"

Although the timing may have been inappropriate, Ali and I doubled over in laughter. Revelin even rolled his eyes and snorted.

"I've seen infants with more wit," Revelin grumbled, though unable to fully hide his smile.

"And I've seen rocks with more emotion," Nico said, his face flushed. "C'mon Revelin, lighten up. You're doing better already."

Thankfully Revelin realized Nico was joking and laughed along with me and Ali. Though his mother's death may haunt him for many years, he was easing back into normalcy.

My gut lurched when I remembered the Deceivers would be coming to take us to the gathering at any moment. "Nico, Revelin, and Ali, we need to talk privately," I said.

Nico's smile disappeared immediately, and I nodded to reassure him I wouldn't be revealing the majority of the plan. We walked to the most secluded corner, still standing but huddling into a tight circle and lowering our voices.

"What's going on?" Revelin, who stood on my left, and Ali, who stood on my right, asked simultaneously. They glanced at each other and Ali blushed.

"Okay, listen carefully," I began, disregarding the awkwardness. "Casimir's going to do *everything* in his power to make sure that the townspeople believe that Cyra is a better ruler than Revelin. He will tie our hands and mouths, making sure we can't protest.

"I don't know why Cyra requested that the four of us be

presented at the gathering, but I can only guess it's because she has a plan. Ali and Revelin, I need you to try to be as submissive and quiet as possible. Revelin, this'll be especially difficult for you, but you *have* to try. If insulted, ignore it. And whatever happens, don't get in Cyra's way. But most importantly…" *run when I tell you to run.*

The end of my sentence was butchered by a horde of about twenty Deceivers storming down the staircase. They burst into the cell, most of them snickering, and used metallic rope to tie firm bonds around each of our hands and in our mouths. The four of us didn't break eye contact; the three of them stared at me while I glanced at each of them. We knew that we had to stay together and be careful.

"Well, well, *well*," Casimir's voice echoed down the staircase, "it's *finally* time. Make sure to expose them to the sunlight *quickly*…maybe it'll blind them. And they'll finally have to deal with what I had to for so many years…the curse of blindness…." He was muttering unimportant things, exposing his uneasiness.

The Deceivers led us out of the cell and up the stairs, and even the dim light of the blue chandelier was bright to my eyes. Casimir stood beside the large front doors, a broad grin stretching his cheeks. Revelin, Nico, Ali, and I remained as calm as possible, trying to eliminate any suspicion the Deceivers might have had. Shamelessly, the Deceivers grabbed each of us around the neck and forced us to line up before the door.

"The people have already gathered, and I've told them Cyra's returning. I told them that reports of her death weren't true…that Timoria and I had been playing with Cyra outside the walls and she ran away into the distance, unable to be found again, so we thought she must've died. They're excited to welcome back the kind, happy, innocent rightful heir," he said, placing his hands on the doorknobs. "Now, welcome once again to daylight."

Ali was quicker than the rest of us and her eyes flew shut just before Casimir flung open the tall doors. The radiant beams of the dying sun sliced through the air and buried painfully into my face. I gasped as my eyes reflexively snapped shut, but I could still see the light against my eyelids. I didn't dare open my eyes again, but I didn't need to. As the Deceivers pushed us out onto the metal ground, my bare feet stepped into what felt like cold feathers. It couldn't have been…not in the middle of warm weather.

Snow.

I could feel the soft, thick flakes floating onto my arms and prickling my face. But I wasn't too surprised: every few years the weather would change drastically and nobody ever knew why. I asked my father once, and he said that he knew the reason why, but he wouldn't tell. I guessed it had to do with the outside world.

The icy air bit into my skin, but I hardly noticed because of the sound of a roaring crowd that bounced across the breeze. My feet were growing numb as we marched forward, and I could hear Casimir barking orders to Deceivers, telling the majority of them to guard me.

"*Open your eyes!*" A Deceiver hissed from beside me.

Gradually my eyes opened, and I was thankful that the sun had mostly disappeared. After a second of blurry eyesight, reality smacked into me as my sight registered a crowd of every single townsperson, jumping and shouting with joy.

It felt as if an ice cube had slipped into my stomach as the Deceivers pushed Revelin, Nico, Ali, and me up a short flight of steps and onto a small metal stage. The Deceivers lined the four of us beside each other at the front of the stage, facing the crowd, and stepped back, making sure to be just inches behind us in case Cyra tried any surprise attacks.

The deafening sounds of the crowd seemed to disappear as I spotted my family off to the right, my parents' faces downcast and Andrew's cheeks wet with tears. I forced myself to look away, knowing I was unable to do anything to be with them.

Most of the townspeople weren't expecting snow, and shivered in their warm weather clothing as they cheered. Breaths from hundreds of mouths gathered like a light fog above the crowd, shifting eerily in the gentle breeze. An elderly man with a cane limped along the edge of the crowd, trying to get closer to the stage. The few Deceivers in the crowd covered their sensitive ears and tried to calm the townspeople.

Ali, Revelin, Nico, and I huddled closer to each other, Ali and I being in the middle. Though my hands were bound, I was able to reach over and squeeze Ali's hand comfortingly. She had been glancing along the outer edges of the crowd, obviously searching for any sign of Cyra, but reassured me with a small smile.

Casimir stepped forward, occupying the few feet of stage just in front of me. His large boots left prints in the snow and the faint glow of the Dream-Catcher reflected off his silvery clothing. The snowflakes whipped through his gray cloak and melted as they were ensnared in his messy hair.

He raised his right hand to shoulder level, bending his fingers forward as if choking someone—the usual gesture he used to silence the crowd. Within half a minute, the townspeople were silent. Casimir allowed the silence to endure for a few seconds, building up the tension.

"The time has come," he began, his deep, loud voice bellowing across the crowd for what seemed like miles, "for Cyra to return. You will welcome her adoringly, for she is my *true* heir."

"How could we *not* welcome her adoringly? She's too sweet!" a middle-aged woman proclaimed from the front of the crowd. A few townspeople cheered in agreement, but Casimir silenced them again.

"*Quiet now!* She'll be arriving at any moment," he said.

I could feel Ali's body shaking beside me as everyone waited eagerly for a person they all thought was kind and innocent, for a person they all remembered as gentle and friendly. I felt trapped standing between Ali and Nico, wanting to do *something*. But I was unable to fall asleep to dream, or attack because my hands were bound. I cast a sidelong glance at Nico, and he nodded subtly. We had to stick to and rely on the plan.

A few minutes passed and the townspeople were growing

doubtful. They whispered to each other as Casimir's confidence dwindled. I searched every corner, shadow, and street within view…but they were unoccupied by the one person we were all looking for. My shoulders slumped a little lower when I noticed the lilac tree, its flowers crumpling and falling with the sudden snow.

The wind twirled thousands of snowflakes, the white flecks capturing the few remaining beams of sunlight. My toes grew numb, my throat constricted, and my stomach felt as if it were full of rocks. Revelin's bright eyes were bloodshot as they raked through the crowd. He stood on the other side of Ali, his posture straight and his chin lifted as if immune to the cold. His breath was labored though…quick and sharp.

What if the plan didn't work? I would have to go back to the cell and create the awful things that Casimir wished so long to have. There was such a slight possibility of the plan's working…it would be foolish to try….

My breath caught when I gazed out at the crowd. The sounds of their whispers, coughs, breaths…all disappeared. I watched them move as if they were figures in one of my dreams, the snow catching in their hair as their eyes were alive with curiosity. There were only a few people out there that I truly cared for, yet *each* person was special. Each of them had a reason to live, try, fail, succeed, fall, stand…yet they weren't able to. They were restrained. They couldn't get outside the walls.

That was why I had to try. Even if they couldn't be given a

chance today, I *knew* I would come back eventually and give them a chance. I would come back…I would.

I saw Louis standing in the center of the crowd, his outline glowing brighter than those around him. *Lilah…* he seemed to say. *Imagination is the key to surviving all that is real.*

But it wasn't.

No, Louis, I wanted to say back to him. But I knew he couldn't hear me. *The imagination you speak of is the key to* hiding *from all that is real. You have to face reality, and if you can do so with the help of imagination, then you have truly found the key.*

Over there, look, look, he said.

I frowned in confusion.

"LOOK, OVER THERE!" a voice shouted from beside me.

I shook my head, surfacing out of a daze. The crowd had fallen into yells and screams of happy disbelief. Revelin, Nico, and Ali started to shuffle away from the front of the stage, but the Deceivers made them stand still. Every eye in the crowd turned and was facing the wall behind them.

Those of us on the stage stared straight ahead. The final, single ray of sunlight gleamed just feet above the wall, outlining a silhouette that stood upon the top of the stones. The crowd erupted into cheers.

"My daughter," Casimir whispered longingly, his face pale.

Surrounded by the warm glow of the setting sun, Cyra stood boldly against the orange sky.

13 The Angel's Ambiguity

Casimir dropped to his knees. Nobody noticed.

Silence quickly devoured the crowd as everyone tried to believe that what they saw before their eyes wasn't an illusion. *Cyra*…the name whispered along the breeze with the snowflakes and into every ear.

Standing upon the wall in the final ray of sunlight, an angelic, stunningly beautiful creature gazed at the crowd. Fragile, translucent-blonde hair tumbled in waves down her pale, elegant skin and a white dress billowed, ghost-like, around her thin frame. Even from a distance I could see her red lips curved into a genuine, warm smile. Her face was young, kind, and *alive*.

Nobody could tear their eyes away as she skillfully climbed down the wall, receiving a few gasps. Her beauty was so intimidating that nobody wanted to move closer, but as she walked toward the stage, the crowd parted to form a path. As she drew nearer, I could see that instead of confidence, she showed shyness.

As Cyra walked onto the stage, casting a glance at me, everything seemed surreal—her eyes were pure white, like two full moons. The non-blind Deceivers instinctively took a step back, some blushing and turning away and others gawking with their mouths drooped open. When she reached Casimir, she extended a pretty arm and helped him onto his feet again.

As if being pushed into icy water, I finally remembered that I was supposed to be engaging in a plan and I turned to face Nico.

He looked as if he had just experienced Casimir leaping through a field of wildflowers and tossing candy in the air.

His jaw dropped to his chest in disbelief and his eyes couldn't have gotten any wider. When Cyra glanced at him, his cheeks and neck turned the brightest color of red and his eye twitched. Annoyance flooded me and I forcefully nudged him with my elbow. He flinched, but I had his attention. I stared at him until he nodded, indicating that he still remembered the plan.

Cyra and Casimir were still looking at each other, exchanging a few words. Casimir couldn't have been happier: he was bubbling with excitement. Cyra was undeniably distracting; her appearance was unlike any other. Her skin seemed to glow as if still holding that final sunray. Her face showed such innocence and kindness…my mind kept twisting, confusing me as to whether or not she was good.

All that Nico and I had to do was to wait: wait for the right moment to fake my death. Nico would take the poison dart we had found on the ground where Lucetta's body was and pretend it had pierced my neck. He would then blame the death on Cyra and we would escape as everyone's attention turned away from us.

Cyra faced the crowd, her mouth parted as if about to speak, but she closed it again. She seemed strangely bashful for someone so bold. Or was she bold? She killed those people, but did she do it on purpose? Maybe she was sorry for doing it. I could have forgiven her, she seemed so innocent.

I shook my head. *No.* What was I thinking?

The crowd noticed her shyness and applauded, encouraging her and cheering her on.

"It's so good to see all of you again," she said, "I-I don't know how to start."

Her voice was quieter than Casimir's…sweet, mesmerizing, gentle…and *genuine.* It carried across the crowd and echoed against the wall. The crowd automatically became happier, as if Cyra was just the way that they remembered her.

Casimir, on the other hand, was frowning. But Cyra turned and whispered a few words to him, and he was grinning again. The sun had disappeared and the sky was black. If it weren't for the dim blue lamppost, nothing could have been seen.

"I want to apologize," she began, "for being away for so long, and for scaring everyone into thinking that I was dead. I would never—I *could* never—leave my people. You're all so *faithful* to me…I truly hope I can fulfill your expectations."

She turned and walked to Revelin, Nico, Ali, and me, her small boot-clad feet leaving prints in the snow. The cold didn't affect her. The hair on my neck prickled as she reached a hand toward me. It first rested on my cheek, and her smile was so comforting that I didn't feel scared.

Earning a gasp from Casimir and every Deceiver on stage, Cyra untied the cloth on my mouth and the bonds on my wrists. They fluttered to my feet, landing in the snow. She then went to Nico, Ali, and Revelin, untying each rope and cloth.

I stared in disbelief at Nico, then at Revelin and Ali. We were too shocked to react. There was no way that our plan could work…Cyra's action was completely unexpected.

But why not just run away? My feet were burning, begging me to escape, but dozens of Deceivers were blocking every direction. Nico looked at me, silently asking what we were supposed to do. But I was utterly lost…no ideas would come to my mind.

Cyra stepped back, allowing the crowd to see the broken bonds, and they erupted into cheers. So this was what she had planned, to trick the townspeople into believing she was kindhearted, that she didn't intend to use me for the purposes Casimir had intended.

But was she actually tricking *the townspeople*? What if she was trying to trick *Casimir* into setting us free? After all, she didn't seem to want to use the Gift for anything. She seemed content with what she already had.

In confusion, the Deceivers naturally stepped closer to me, making it impossible for me to move. Casimir was dumbfounded, but Cyra whispered a few more words into his ear and he relaxed again.

"C'mon Dad, did you *really* have to tie them up?" Cyra said loudly, making the crowd burst into laughter.

Casimir blushed and shrugged. That was when I knew that something was *very* wrong. Cyra must have been twisting minds. Everything seemed so much the opposite: the opposite of what I expected…the opposite of what I had always known. Nico, Revelin, and Ali sensed it too. They looked at each other in discomfort and then searched for escape routes.

Sensing our discomfort, Cyra sighed. "It's alright," she said quietly so that only the four of us could hear, "Really, it's okay. I'm not going to let him use you. I'll show him that he can be happy with what he already has."

I was speechless.

My mind was grinding like two rocks rubbing together. Revelin stumbled back a little from his rigid stance…he also didn't know what to believe. Nico and Ali each grabbed one of my wrists, their fingers digging into my skin. *What do we do*? they seemed to ask. *WHAT IS GOING ON?*

Cyra faced the crowd again. "Let's change this. Dad, look how much your people admire you. How much *I* admire you. Look at your palace, your faithful Deceivers….You *already have* everything that'll make you truly happy. You don't need Lilah's dreams."

Casimir frowned, glancing at me and Cyra. Finally he nodded, accepting that what Cyra said was true. The townspeople cheered with such happiness that some of them began to cry. It could have started snowing bricks and I wouldn't have been as shocked as I was right then.

"She's changed him!" One townsperson shouted.

A few of the Deceivers clapped, but the rest were shaking their heads in disagreement and confusion. I drew closer to Nico, Ali, and Revelin, having a strange feeling that something drastic was about to happen.

Casimir continued to nod and pretended to cry as Cyra sympathetically hugged him. What she then did was so quick that if I blinked, or breathed, I would have missed it.

Still hugging Casimir, Cyra's bony, nimble fingers glided up to his neck with a natural movement and something needle-like slid from her hand and pierced his skin. She gently released herself from the hug, discreetly tucking the needle-like object into her dress and out of sight.

I then noticed it was one of her poison darts.

And there, along the side of one of her legs, I saw the thinnest bulge which must have been a dart-gun.

She acted as if nothing had happened. She faced the crowd again and lifting her hands into the air, received screams of appreciation. I looked at the Deceivers, but most were blind and hadn't seen. I looked at Nico, Revelin, and Ali, and their faces were just as dark as mine.

The four of us were the only ones who had seen Cyra's murder.

I felt as if I had been punched in the stomach.

I *knew*. I *knew* Cyra wanted me. She wanted me just for herself. She wanted to take me to the outside world, secluding the two of us. Using me for only *her* desires. This was all an act, an act to gain everyone's trust, and then disappear with me sometime in the shadows of night.

The air had been so warm with joy that it could have melted the snow, but within seconds the joy was doused.

Casimir's smile disappeared as he stared at his daughter. With a single, shaky hand, he slowly stroked the smallest slit on his neck. A few drops of glistening blood trickled from the wound and dropped into the snow. His cheeks paled and his eyes rolled around as he fell to his knees, landing with a bone-snapping crunch.

His body swayed left and then right until he plummeted face-first into the snow at Cyra's feet.

Everything was happening too quickly for it to register with me.

"And I promise to always protect—" Cyra said to the crowd, pausing when she saw Casimir, "—D-Dad?!"

Cyra's dramatic entrance had been achieved. The crowd was reduced to silence as she knelt beside Casimir, her face holding the most genuine expressions of fear and pain. Tears began pouring from her eyes…she was *really* upset that her father had died. It was almost as if she didn't know she had just killed him.

The Deceivers all around me foolishly scrambled to gather around Casimir, the non-blind ones explaining to the others what they thought had happened. Cyra rolled Casimir onto his back, placing a hand on his heart as if feeling his pulse. Nobody dared interrupt her. She looked so fragile.

I stared at Revelin, remembering that Casimir was his *father*. A breath escaped me when I realized both of his parents had been killed within days of each other…and by the same person.

Cyra.

A single scream shattered the silence. *"DAD! No, no, NO!"* Cyra wailed. *"Call for help…someone please!"*

The crowd stood frozen with fear, the townspeople confusedly blinking and gasping…unsure of what to do.

My stomach boiled with anger. Everyone was being fed with Cyra's lies, and everyone believed them. Revelin's face was red, his fists were clenched, and he breathed so heavily that thick clouds formed in the cold air.

"I'm really sorry," a townsperson shouted. "But at least now Cyra's our leader!"

The Deceivers were still angry and shocked, but the townspeople gradually cheered again. They never loved Casimir and would happily accept Cyra.

I couldn't wait any longer; I needed to reveal the truth to everyone. Cyra had to be stopped. I stepped to the front of the stage and everyone was too muddled to stop or notice me. The words were just forming in my throat when a familiar voice yelled across the crowd.

"CYRA LIES!" Louis howled.

Cyra looked up with tears in her eyes and every Deceiver was prepared to pounce on Louis. But Louis wasn't the only person who could see through the deceit. My mother and father, Nico's parents, a few other people, and even Ali's mentally-abused parents joined in Louis's chants.

"CYRA LIES! CYRA LIES! CYRA LIES!"

Tension was building like a hungry fire. Some Deceivers moved into the crowd, headed for my parents with nightsticks; but in an effort to protect, a few townspeople blocked their way. Voices rose and Cyra knew she was losing everyone's attention.

"I'm so sorry..." Cyra coughed through her tears. "How could I lie? *Why* would I lie? What is there to lie about? Oh, I didn't want anyone to get angry."

Revelin's last thread of restraint had been severed.

He lunged toward Cyra with such strength that five Deceivers lost their balance and toppled into the snow. As if expecting him, Cyra managed to stand. But Revelin dove and knocked her down onto the stage before she could react.

With her quick reflexes, Ali reached down to the startled Deceivers and took their nightsticks. She grabbed one firmly in her hand and tossed two others to me and Nico. The Deceivers had regained their feet and were headed for Revelin, but Nico, Ali, and I stepped in their way.

By that time the crowd had lost most of its sanity and had no idea which side to take. Some joined my parents and Louis, charging in hordes toward Deceivers, either trampling them or being killed by them. Some were on Cyra's side, edging closer to the stage and even attacking those townspeople that cursed the angelic heir.

The nightstick felt unfamiliar in my hand, but I somehow easily became accustomed to it. A woman Deceiver swung her fist at my face, but I sidestepped just in time and returned it with a lucky blow to the forehead. She wobbled before falling at my feet, unconscious.

It took me a moment to register what I had done, but another Deceiver was charging at me before I could take a breath. The other dozen Deceivers that were on the stage had plunged into the crowd some time ago, so only seven remained. Nico was fighting with one who still had a nightstick while Ali dodged in around him and struck piercing stabs into the side of his foe.

As the charging Deceiver's nightstick clashed with my own, I noticed Revelin pinning Cyra to the stage. Cyra used one hand to whip the blow-gun out from underneath her dress, but Revelin cleverly smacked it from her grip as she tried to pull out poison darts with the other hand.

In her half-second of confusion, he quickly knocked the darts away. Cyra took advantage of that and glided out from under Revelin as if made of water. She took the one poison dart from her dress that she had used to kill Casimir, holding it like a knife as she stared down her target.

In the few seconds I took to watch Revelin, I received a hit to my right rib. Pain shattered through my body, making me yelp. All air escaped my lungs, but I raised my nightstick just before the Deceiver hit me on the other side.

Hot tears stung my eyes, but I forced them back. I couldn't

afford blurry vision. This Deceiver was bigger than the others on stage. He was trying not to hurt me too badly because of the Gift, but he was definitely trying to restrain me as much as possible.

I stumbled back to catch a breath, clutching my rib, and the Deceiver saw his chance. He leaped forward, grasping my arm. I struggled but knew his strength was greater than mine. He took some rope from his belt, preparing to tie me, but Ali appeared.

She picked up a spare nightstick from the snow and hurled it through the air. It flashed horridly with the blue light of the lamppost before crushing the Deceiver's skull with a crunch. There wasn't even enough time for me to see if he was dead.

One of the Deceivers on stage had found the dart-gun and was aiming at Nico. I dove for her, knocking her aim askew, and the dart lodged into the arm of the Deceiver fighting Nico. A trail of blood trickled from the puncture and he collapsed into the snow.

The Deceiver beside me with the dart gun yelled and reached for me. They *knew* that they *could not* let me escape.

Without thinking I ducked and crawled between her legs, grabbing one of her ankles so that she stumbled forward. Nico appeared and pushed her off the stage. She fell into the crowd, lost from our sight.

The few remaining Deceivers charged but Ali and Nico guarded me from them. Normally the Deceivers would have demolished their small, young opponents, but they had to be careful not to hurt them too badly. Especially *valuable prisoners* like me and my friends.

I turned to Cyra and Revelin, but they were moving too quickly for me to intervene. I then looked at the crowd.

Whatever kind of battle this was, we were losing.

The Deceivers in the crowd were overtaking the townspeople. Their metal nightsticks flew in every direction, trying not to kill, but accidentally taking some lives.

Then, I saw my father, shoving through the people and closer to the stage. His gaze was locked on me and he opened his mouth to speak, but a Deceiver grabbed him from behind, thinking he intended to go after Cyra. He was dragged back into the crowd, yelling words I could hardly hear, but one came out clearly.

"DAYDREAM!"

I was too distracted to think straight. But somehow, his order made sense. *Daydream.*

Avoiding another pounce from a Deceiver, I made for Casimir's body. My numb feet felt as if they were no longer there as I slid through the snow and kneeled beside the dead leader. The blood around the wound in his neck was starting to freeze.

Within seconds I found what I was looking for. I yanked the Dream-Catcher from Casimir's neck and leaped back from his body. Cyra had seen me.

After deflecting an attack from Revelin, she gazed at me with a sympathetic frown. She looked *sorry.* Sorry that any of this had happened. My mind twisted...I *knew* she was trying to trick me. But what if it wasn't her fault? She had been locked away for so many years that it must have damaged her, and she didn't know that it was wrong to kill. She acted on impulse and regretted it; I could see it in her eyes.

"She's deceiving you!" Revelin screamed.

As if dunked in icy water I shook my head and turned to Revelin. Cyra's frown flashed to a glare as she made another attempt to stab her brother. Her movements were quick and skilled as if expertly trained, but Revelin's reflexes were just as swift.

Daydream.

My father's order echoed through me as I stood up. Nico and Ali were still distracting the few Deceivers on stage, but some of the Deceivers in the crowd were sprinting toward me. They must have just remembered that *I* was the person they had to keep from escaping.

Daydream. I faced away from everything, staring down at the snow. It should be easy…I had done it many times before in school.

I clenched my fists and released them. I inhaled a slow breath, making my stomach settle. My eyes gradually closed. I could hear Cyra yelling behind me and the footsteps from the Deceivers in the crowd getting closer.

Dozens of feet slapped the stairs that led onto the stage…I would be surrounded in seconds. My senses became hazy and I could feel the Dream-Catcher faintly vibrating against my chest.

The Deceivers reached me. Hands grabbed my shoulders, wrists, and legs. Ali screamed. But *no*. I wouldn't let them capture us this time.

Reality disappeared like a crack of lightning. I hadn't planned a dream; I could only hope it would save us. In a few seconds, a picture flashed before my mind's eye. Nico, Revelin, Ali, and I were standing on top of the stone wall beside the solid metal gate.

Reality returned quicker than it had disappeared. My eyes flew open.

The first thing I registered was the noise of the crowd...it was in the distance. I was staring forward, but the thing before my eyes made no connection with my mind. I then noticed a hand grabbing my arm and my stomach dropped, as I thought it was a Deceiver.

"LILAH!" Ali's voice shouted.

I drew in a sharp breath, snowflakes catching in my throat. I looked down and nearly lost my balance. It was just like my dream. Nico, Ali, Revelin, and I were standing side-by-side on top of the wall.

14 First Breath

"Revelin, Nico, Lilah…COME ON!" Ali urged.

The stone wall beneath my feet was about six feet thick but I felt as if I were standing on a wire. The daydream had sapped some of my energy and I wobbled, trying to keep my balance. Ali was sitting on the edge of the wall, facing into the unknown area. The area outside of the walls.

It looked so different from what I imagined. Fields and small snow-covered hills stretched on as far as I could see, and trees were scattered across the ground. The sky was grayish-black but there must have been a full moon because the brightness was such that everything could be seen.

Nico, Revelin, and I were still in shock. I had no idea how Ali could adjust to surprises as quickly as she did. She was urging us to climb down the wall. We had to leave immediately…the Deceivers must have been searching the town and might spot us at any second.

My numb hands and feet gripped the stones as much as possible. The wall was impossible to climb from the inside because the stones were so smooth, but on the outside they were more rigid.

The four of us carefully descended the wall just as the yells of Deceivers reached our ears. Luckily they hadn't seen us.

We were just feet from the ground when Ali slipped from the wall and fell into the snow. I noticed her arm was bleeding as she struggled to sit up. When my feet touched the earth I couldn't feel it. My fingers and toes were numb.

"Ali…Ali are you alright?" I said.

Nico and Revelin had reached the ground and were standing beside me. We helped Ali onto her feet. There was a gash along her upper arm where a Deceiver must have hit her.

"I'm fine, it's okay," she squeaked. But I knew she was hurt and needed a bandage.

The snow was half-a-foot deep but it was falling quickly. It would be up to our knees by morning.

But *where* would we go?

We had no food, shelter, shoes… We hadn't eaten a satisfying meal in months. We would freeze to death in a few hours or starve. We didn't even know if there were any people close by…or if they would even be willing to help us. They might think we were thieves or murderers and wouldn't take us in.

Lost for ideas, I looked at Revelin. He hadn't spoken in a while but his eyes were glowing with adrenaline.

"I know what we have to do," he said. "C'mon, see that light on top of the hill? We need to get there. But first we have to hide. Quick, go behind that tree."

Without question the four of us started pushing through the

snow, going toward a large, bare tree. As we ducked behind it, my ribcage stung and I remembered how the Deceiver had hit me. Revelin noticed me flinch but I shook my head and pretended the pain wasn't there.

The four of us sat silently behind the tree, staring at the metal gate. The stone wall was so tall that it concealed the entire town from view except for the tips of Casimir's palace at the far edge. I couldn't help but wonder *why* nobody in the outside world had ever seen it before and tried to get inside.

We waited without speaking for what felt like half-an-hour until the metal doors cracked open and a single non-blind Deceiver stepped out. He was about twenty yards away from our tree but he didn't walk around or search.

His eyes were squinted as he stared in every direction. He must have not been intelligent enough to look for footprints in the snow. He turned and shrugged to someone who was standing inside the doors.

"There isn't anyone out here," the Deceiver said.

"NO!" Cyra's voice exclaimed from the other side of the doors. I couldn't see her, but her voice was loud. "How didn't anyone see her? She shouldn't have been able to close her eyes for even a *second*! You know how powerful her dreams can be! She just disappeared. She, Revelin, Ali, and Nico…they were there on stage; then they just *disappeared* into thin air. They could be *anywhere* by now. ANYWHERE."

"I-I'm sorry…I…They probably haven't left the town," the

Deceiver said. "How could Lilah dream herself *outside* of the town if she doesn't know what it *looks like* outside of the town? It's impossible."

"No, I'm sorry for being angry. You just don't understand," Cyra said with a sugary voice. "Gather a search group and we'll set off as soon as possible."

The Deceiver grinned, nodded, and went back through the metal doors, securely shutting them behind him.

I looked at Revelin, Nico, and Ali…we were all exhausted. We had to move quickly or Cyra's search group would catch up to us. I tried to urge them to move, but Ali was slowly losing consciousness. Her small limbs were turning purple from the cold and her eyes had fluttered shut. The blood from the gash on her arm had frozen.

Nico was frantically trying to keep her awake. His lips were white and his body shook with shivers. He kept lightly smacking Ali's face so that she jolted in and out of consciousness.

Revelin's face was twisted in strange angles as he sat alone with his arms crossed. I could tell that so many disturbing thoughts were racing through his mind. The death of his father and mother…his corrupt sister…the great possibility of his going mad because it ran in the family. He shivered violently and seemed lost for ideas. The light on the hill was far away…there was no way we would make it.

I settled into a crooked root in the tree. My feet were swollen and turning darker in color. We had to get out of the snow right then or else permanent damage would be done to our bodies.

I knew what had to be done.

"Ali, Revelin, Nico…" I said. "It's okay. We'll make it."

The Dream-Catcher dangled loosely against my gray tunic. The metallic strings glowed and hummed as if aware of what I was about to do. I allowed my heavy eyelids to fall and I pictured the four of us standing just in front of the light on the hill.

I fell into a dream and was jolted awake a minute later by Revelin shaking my shoulders. My eyes focused on his face and he was smiling for the first time in days.

"Lilah you did it, look!" he said.

He moved aside and just in front of me was a warm, bright light from inside a little house. A sigh of relief and a little laugh escaped my mouth. I looked back and could see the smallest dot in the distance which must have been the stone wall. There was no way that Cyra could reach us anytime soon.

My moment of happiness disappeared when I looked at Ali. Her breathing was slow and Nico couldn't get her eyes to open.

"Hurry, we have to get inside," I said.

"But who knows what could be in there?" Nico hesitated, not moving from the spot.

"Whatever's in there is better than whatever's out here," Revelin said. "We won't last out here much longer. I doubt that anything inside that house will try to kill us."

"It doesn't matter, Ali's fading. We need to get her inside *now*," I ordered.

Nico nodded and Revelin helped him to pick up Ali. They carried her behind me as I walked closer to the house.

It looked almost abandoned. It was made of mossy stone but was well built and had a strong roof. There were no other houses or signs of life anywhere that I could see, but a small road with what looked like thick carriage-tracks led from the side of the house into the distance.

"I think those are tire tracks from a car," Nico pointed out. "Louis drew a picture of them once."

"Then somebody definitely lives here," I said. "But it looks like they aren't home right now."

I neared the green front door and placed my hand on the doorknob. My stomach churned…this was all strange and felt wrong. What if *people* didn't live outside of the walls…what if they were some sort of strange creature? What if a killer lived inside the house?

I heard Ali whimper and pushed all fear aside. The door was unlocked and I cautiously pushed it open.

Heat came billowing through the air and warmed my face. Electrical light from bulbs like those in Casimir's palace were held in strange objects on tables. But the light wasn't blue; it was yellowish. *Lamps* Louis said they were called.

Not looking at my surroundings, I stepped inside and Revelin and Nico followed, careful not to hit Ali against the doorframe. I closed the door behind them and slowly turned around. Everywhere I looked, there were too many weird objects for me to think about. So I ignored them and helped lower Ali onto a couch in front of a fireplace.

Luckily a warm fire was radiating heat throughout the room and instantly I felt a good tingling sensation in my feet. The couch was long so Revelin sat beside Ali, stretching out his feet so that they were closer to the fire.

Nico wasn't comfortable, though. His red-rimmed eyes glanced around the room.

"I'm going to have a look around; I want to make sure that nobody's home," he said. He wandered into a room that looked like the kitchen then quietly disappeared up a flight of stairs.

The house was so small that there were no walls dividing the rooms, and there was only a kitchen beside the room where Revelin, Ali, and I were. I didn't know what was upstairs but I could only guess the bedrooms.

Now that my adrenaline was almost gone, the pain on my ribcage was getting stronger and I felt drained from dreaming twice in a short amount of time. But it didn't matter; I would be fine. Ali's health was what needed attention.

I went over to Ali and kneeled beside her. The color was returning to her skin and her breathing was at a normal rate. Her eyes opened a little and she smiled when she saw my face.

"You really did it, Lilah. We escaped all because of you. But where are we now?" she said.

"But we also got *into* this mess because of me," I said in an apologetic tone. "And remember that light we saw on the hill? It was too far away to walk so I dreamed us here. You were unconscious. But now it's okay; we're in an empty house. I don't really know *where* we are, but it seems safe."

She nodded, slowly falling asleep. I noticed the gash on her arm again and asked Revelin to look for a bandage. He rummaged around the kitchen and came back in a few minutes with a towel. As Ali fell into a deep sleep, I wiped off some of the blood and wrapped the wound.

Relieved, Nico returned and told us the house was empty. We were hungry, but too tired to look for food. We didn't know when the person who lived in the house would be back, but we didn't really care. We needed to rest at least until sunrise.

The three of us lay down on the soft, fur-covered floor in front of the fire. A *rug* was what Louis called it.

Louis…I hoped he, my family, and the other townspeople were alright. I wouldn't let myself think of them. There wasn't anything I could do to help them. If I dreamed them outside of the walls, other townspeople would be questioned and punished. As my father said, it was best not to use the Gift.

I needed to sleep but dreaded having to wake every hour. Right then I wished more than ever that I could sleep a full night without having to wake myself up. I turned my head to look at Nico but he was already fast asleep. Revelin was on the other side of me and I faced him. He was wide awake. He was lying on his back, staring at the ceiling. His face was still twisted as unpleasant thoughts crowded his mind.

"I know where we are," he said quietly, not tearing his gaze from the ceiling.

"How could you possibly know that?" I asked softly, trying to stay awake.

He rotated his head to look at me then lifted his hand to show me something. There, resting on his palm, was something that looked like a very detailed drawing. He explained that he had found it in the kitchen. I think it was a *photograph*. It had color and looked *so* real. It was a picture of a young couple standing in front of a gigantic structure.

Revelin flipped over the picture and on the back was a short message written beautifully in golden letters. It was written in a strange language, but there were a few words in the corner I could read.

Saint Basil's Cathedral, Russia.

"Russia?" I said. "Louis mentioned something about this place before. I think it's near his home, France."

Revelin nodded. "There's something I know that I've never told anyone. Something that I heard my father talking about."

I nodded, waiting for him to tell me.

"You know how the weather changes drastically throughout the years? It's because…it's because the town *moves*. Whenever somebody in the outside world sees it, it moves to a different rural location so that it can never be discovered," he said.

"So all this time you *knew* why people from the outside world hadn't discovered us," I said in slight annoyance. "But how did Casimir make it so that the town can move like that?"

"My dad didn't do it. When your great-grandfather was on his deathbed, my great-grandfather found him. Your great-grandfather was forced to dream that the town would never be found by other people, so he dreamed that the town could *move*. My great-grandfather wanted to be sure that the Gift would always be within his possession and nobody else's."

I released a breath, the concept too mystifying for me to question. But there was one thing that didn't make sense to me. "How did Casimir manage to get supplies and food from the outside world?"

Revelin's electric eyes flickered. "My father was a thief and a murderer. Every time he left the town, he went into villages and farms and stole as much food and necessities as available. If anyone protested, the Deceivers threatened to kill."

Fresh anger flooded my stomach…Casimir spent so much effort and so many lives just to find the Gift. So many precious things wasted for personal desires. It wasn't a surprise that Revelin wasn't too depressed about his father's death.

"Lilah, I need to ask you something," Revelin said nervously, changing the subject.

"Of course," I said, completely unaware of what he was thinking.

"Do you think that I'm…I mean…" he stuttered. He was having great difficulty speaking. "Do you think that I could turn out like Cyra? After all she *was* kindhearted when she was younger, but then she changed. When I was on stage fighting her…she was so much like my dad. She was trying to *kill* me.

"Yeah I was angry that she *murdered our parents* and was deceiving the townspeople, but I would never kill her. I just…I don't think I'd want to live if I had to be like them." He spoke quickly as if wanting to get it over with.

We stared at each other for a while and I sighed. "Do you know that this is the first time you've ever questioned yourself?" I said, pointing out his past big-headed personality.

He smiled a little. "Yeah I guess it is."

"Well…you say that Cyra changed, but people don't really *change*. They *develop*. Cyra is still the same girl that she was as a child, but her underlying, true personality came out as an adult. You're already seventeen, and you're *nothing* like Cyra and Casimir. You're like Lucetta, full of…*light*."

Revelin's eyes softened as he smiled at me; then he blushed as he turned to look at the ceiling again. That must have been the first time I saw him truly blush. After a minute, he spoke again.

"Is it what you always thought it was going to be like?" he asked.

"Freedom?" I replied. I knew he was referring to escaping the town.

"Yeah," he said, his voice getting quieter.

"Not exactly…it all happened too fast. But most good things happen too fast. And the hardest thing is figuring out how to slow them down."

"But that's what makes good things special. We have to chase after them. I'm always having to chase after you," he said so quietly I could hardly hear.

My eyebrows rose in surprise as I turned to look at him, but he was fast asleep. In the moment I couldn't stop myself…it was as if a gust of wind pushed me. My body lifted slightly from the floor and my lips massaged into his. Warmth crackled through me like lightning. I lingered but then quickly drew away, blood rushing to my cheeks.

Revelin's eyes were still closed, but as I turned my head to peer through the window, I thought I saw the smallest smile emerge right where I kissed him.

I sighed a little as I gazed at the moon outside. It was one of those nights—one of those velvet nights when one couldn't help but gaze, mesmerized, at the horizon…and reminisce their past, as well as the past of all humanity.

I knew that I would have to go back and rescue my family and the townspeople. The couple who lived in the house could return at any moment, and Cyra and the Deceivers could reach us by noon tomorrow. But at that moment it didn't matter. At that moment we were free.

www.ingramcontent.com/pod-product-compliance
Lightning Source LLC
Chambersburg PA
CBHW061147170626
46809CB00003B/1016